"So, Washashore, why are you here on the Island?" Beth asked.

"Why does anybody move anywhere?" Clem answered. "Because it seems like a nice place to live."

"That's what all the washashores say."

Clem had always felt at home on the Vineyard. **Like she belonged here.**

But Beth's words made her feel like **she didn't belong *anywhere*.**

Praise for **Washashore**

"*A love story surrounded by this beautiful island—Martha's Vineyard—with its fragile shores and enduring birds. A tender-hearted story that calls out to save what we love so much.*"

Carly Simon,
Grammy Award-winning singer & songwriter

"*The prose brings to life the era of the 1970s, but Goldsmith's themes are timeless and will resonate with teens and adults alike.*"

Lisa Klein,
Award-winning author of *Ophelia,*
Lady MacBeth'sDaughter and *Cate of the Lost Colony*

"*An adventure story in every sense of the word—the adventure, especially, of coming of age on an aging planet.*"

Bill McKibben,
Founder, 350.org and author of *Eaarth,*
The End of Nature and *Deep Economy*

For Dan —

With many thanks for your support of an aspiring fellow author.

Washashore

Suzanne Goldsmith

Suzanne Goldsmith

Lucky Marble Books

An Imprint of PageSpring Publishing

Lucky Marble Books is an imprint of PageSpring Publishing.

Cover illustration copyright © 2013 by PageSpring Publishing.

First printing, 2013

ISBN: 978-1-939403-12-4

Printed in the United States by Lucky Marble Books, an imprint of PageSpring Publishing.
www.luckymarblebooks.com

Ordering Information:
Quantity sales: Special discounts are available on quantity purchases by corporations, associations, and others. For details, contact the publisher at sales@pagespringpublishing.com.
Orders by U.S. trade bookstores and wholesalers: Please contact the publisher at sales@pagespringpublishing.com.

Cover illustration by Chelsea Castillo
Cover design by Sarah Allgire
Interior design by K.A. Matthews

Interior typefaces include *Garamond*, *Nyala*, *Monotype Corsiva*, and *Spicy Rice*

For Dennis

CONTENTS

Acknowledgments   *xi*

1   On Martha's Vineyard   1

2   Birkenstocks and Candie's   9

3   Sunshine Girl   19

4   Birds of North America   26

5   Bird Boy   35

6   You Haven't Seen Her Lately   46

7   More about the Ospreys   53

8   He Belongs to Himself   61

9   Cicada in a Jar   69

10   Something to Look Forward To   78

11   Quitsa's Bands   88

12   Happy Thanksgiving   99

13   Here for the Holiday   107

14   A Reluctant Activist   114

15   You Understand, Don't You?   123

16   Sugar Helps   128

17   No Place Like Home   136

18	Merry Christmas	142
19	A Feeling of Safety	151
20	Anyone Like You	160
21	Thank You for Your Interest	167
22	A Crack in the Wall	175
23	City Girl	178
24	What's Fun to Do Around Here?	187
25	We Have to Go	195
26	Speak Up, Miss Harper	201
27	Unbelievable	211
28	Are You Awake Now?	219
29	No Answer	224
30	Emergency	231
31	Nobody Knew	234
32	Like You Could Walk on Water	245
33	We Need to Talk	252
34	Right Here	256
35	How Mother Nature Made Us	261
36	Song of Spring	269
	A Note from the Author	276

ACKNOWLEDGMENTS

I would like to thank the members of my writing posse, the Wordshop, who for many years have nurtured this book and my publishing aspirations. I'll never know if I *could* have done it without you, but I am quite certain I *wouldn't* have done it without you. I owe a huge debt to editor Katherine Matthews, who made this book much, much better. I offer thanks to my parents, who brought me to Martha's Vineyard and instilled in me a desire to protect it. And finally—but most importantly—I am grateful to my wonderful husband Dennis Hirsch and our children, Clara and Zander. They have believed in this project, and in me, from the start. Their support has meant everything.

1

On Martha's Vineyard

The first night Clementine Harper spent alone in the cottage was the longest. She ate leftover rice and beans for dinner, washed her dishes, and finished her math homework. Then she put a Cat Stevens album on the turntable, cranked up the volume, and lay down on the couch. She could never play her music this loud when Nora was at home.

But when the record ended and all she could hear was the hiss of the needle sliding across the vinyl and thudding against the label, it was still only eight o'clock. She wasn't the least bit tired. So she called Coco. They'd been best friends ever since they'd met three years ago, in sixth grade.

"I think you're brave," said Coco. "I'd be scared to stay all by myself in a tiny cabin in the woods on some island."

"It is a little weird," Clem admitted, twisting the curly phone cord around her thumb. She sat on the bare wood floor of her new bedroom with the old black phone next to her. "But Nora's just in Boston for one night." Clem called both her parents by their first names. They wanted her to feel like an equal member of the family—although it didn't always work that way. "And she's going to call and check on me before bed."

"Do the doors lock? Aren't you worried about axe murderers?" Coco went to way too many horror movies.

"Of course the doors lock. But we don't usually bother. And I don't think there are any axe murderers on Martha's Vineyard."

"You never know. Someone could be creeping around the woods right now."

She shivered a little. "Cut it out, Coco." Maybe she would lock up before bed.

Clem knew she was young to be staying home alone overnight. But she didn't have any choice. Her dad, Adam, had moved to Ohio to teach for a year at a college there. Her mom still worked at a university in Boston, near Cambridge. They could only afford one apartment, so Nora and Clem had given up their place and moved to Nora's family cottage on Martha's Vineyard, where they could live for free.

But this meant Nora had to go back to Boston to teach for one day every week. She had to ride the ferry, take a two-hour bus ride, teach all day, sleep on a friend's lumpy couch, and then travel all the way back to the Island. So Clem had decided she wouldn't complain about staying alone for one night.

"I like the quiet. And I like being alone. I can stay up all night if I feel like it."

"That sounds cool," said Coco. "I'd kill for that. My parents would never let me stay alone overnight."

"I don't blame them," Clem laughed. "You're a wild child."

"Who, me?" Coco replied. "Well . . . maybe a little."

Clem could almost see her friend's mischievous grin.

Coco loved to complain, but they both knew she liked to push the limits. She played her disco music loud and loved to wear giant earrings, too-short cutoffs, and tight tube tops. She missed curfew all the time. Sometimes Clem thought that if her parents weren't so tough on her, Coco might be doing worse things. Last year, some kids at her middle school dropped acid. One high-school girl had run away to join the Hare Krishnas.

But maybe Coco wouldn't do any of those things. She liked her comfort. At this moment, Clem knew, Coco was reclining on her silky purple quilt, cradling her princess phone and painting her toenails. Clem had been to Coco's apartment a million times, so it was easy for her to imagine Coco now—even though Coco was back at home in Cambridge.

Even though they were separated by eighty miles of highway and a sliver of ocean.

"Do you have a TV, at least?" Coco asked.

3

"We brought one out here once, but the antenna didn't work. It's funny, I don't really miss it . . . at least not that much."

Coco groaned. "I would die without my *Soul Train* fix! But you—I can see you without a TV. You'd probably do okay in a teepee or a mud hut, reading by candlelight."

"Well, we *do* have electricity," Clem said. "A stereo, even. It's Martha's Vineyard, not *Gilligan's Island*."

Coco laughed.

Clem leaned back against the bed. The tiny room had a twin bed with a gray wool blanket stretched tight across it, a nightstand, a battered wooden desk, and a single paint-by-numbers beach scene on the wall.

The digital clock on her desk read 8:11 p.m. She hated that clock because the little numbers flipped by too quickly whenever she talked to Coco on the phone. They'd already been talking for eleven minutes, and Clem was only allowed thirty minutes total for the whole week. Long distance calls were expensive.

"We can't talk much longer. Nora's going to call at exactly 8:30 p.m. to check up on me."

"Does Adam call you, too?"

"Sometimes . . . I miss him," Clem sighed. "It would be so much better if he'd just stayed."

"My dad said, 'You gotta go where the jobs are.'"

"But there must have been something else he could do in Boston, so he wouldn't have to leave me and Nora. He doesn't have to teach college. He could teach school!"

"Wouldn't you die if you ended up in his class?" Coco said.

"Yeah, probably. But couldn't he be a banker or an accountant or something?"

"Your dad is too cool for those jobs, Clem. You're lucky. My dad is so boring."

Was Adam cool? Clem had never really thought of her father like that. Some of his hippie ways were annoying: his long hair, his earring, and the way he went barefoot everywhere, with his embarrassing hairy feet. He used words like "bread" for money and called Nora "Babe."

At least he *used* to call her that.

But maybe he was a little bit cool. He understood things. If Clem tried to tell Adam something that was hard to explain, he always figured out what she was trying to say. He got her. With Nora, she had to spell things out.

"So tell me about school," she said. "I can't believe I'm missing out on freshman year."

"Well, I can't be bothered with ninth grade guys," Coco said, quickly moving to her favorite subject. "Especially the ones I've known forever. It's hard to get interested in any boy you saw in second grade with snot running down his face."

"Oh, nice thought." Clem made a gagging sound.

5

"They look like little kids next to the junior and senior guys." Coco smacked her lips.

Clem giggled.

"What about your little island school? Anyone interesting?"

"Oh, geez. Classes just started last week." Clem lay back on the floor. "The boys seem kind of . . . younger. You know what I mean?"

"I guess we grow up fast here in the big city," said Coco.

"I guess so," said Clem.

They both laughed.

Clem glanced at the clock. "Listen, Coco—I have to go. I don't want Nora to flip out when she sees the phone bill."

"All right, but hey—I want some real news next time."

"I'll work on that. You call me next, okay? Soon?"

"Sure. You got it. Good night, John-Boy."

"Good night, Mary Ellen." Their little joke. That was how every segment of *The Waltons* ended.

"I miss you," said Coco.

"Yeah." Clem's voice cracked a little. "Me, too."

Later, after Nora's call, Clem lay in bed trying to sleep. The cottage seemed even darker and quieter than usual. The room felt chilly. Clem pulled her quilt higher.

If she were still living in Boston, she and Coco would have

spent tonight planning their weekend. They would have talked about shopping for second-hand jeans in Harvard Square and buying records at the Coop and eating sandwiches on the grass in Harvard Yard, trying to look like college students.

Something tapped against the window.

Clem froze. She had no idea where the nearest human was. You couldn't even see another house—and the neighbors were summer people, anyway, surely gone by now. If something happened, who would she call?

Slowly, she turned her head to look at the window. A pine tree branch rubbed against the glass. The tips of the branch scratched the window like fingers.

The wind was picking up. What if there was a hurricane? A power outage? Or a fire?

The fire station was miles away. How would the rescue truck find the house, down all these dirt roads? Or what if she fell off her bike tomorrow and broke a leg when nobody was around to help? How long would it take before people knew she was missing?

Had Nora and Adam thought of any of these things?

Clem reached down and turned on the little nightlight next to the bed. She pulled the blanket tighter and turned toward the wall. She spotted a daddy longlegs slowly making his way across the windowsill. He stopped and patted the window with his thin legs. Was he looking for a way out? She thought of plucking him up by a leg and carrying him outside, but her bed was cozy and she didn't want to get up. Maybe he liked the shelter of the house. She touched his leg very gently with a finger and the spider froze in place.

He was still for a long, long time.

2

Birkenstocks and Candie's

"Hey, Washashore!"

Clem sat eating lunch on the grass, reading a book Adam had given her before he went away. She hesitated for a moment before looking up. A girl in her grade named Beth perched on the guard rail by the school parking lot. Beth was big—not fat but tall and solid, with a wide face. Her long blond hair hung down like straw.

Beth jerked her chin up at Clem. "Yeah, you. You in the Birkenstocks."

Clem closed the book, slowly balled up her sandwich wrap, and put it in her empty brown bag. She got up and brushed the crumbs off her T-shirt and shorts, and then walked over to Beth, who stared at her.

Clem had moved three times in her life, and each time there

9

had been someone like Beth. Someone who thought it was her job to give newcomers a hard time.

"I heard they don't shave their legs in France," said Beth. "Is that the style in Cambridge, too?"

Clem looked down at her bare legs, with their light golden fuzz. Other girls her age shaved. Coco had been shaving since she was eleven.

"My hair is sooo dark, I've got no choice," Coco had said, pointing at her wild black curls. "I'd look like a bear. You should be glad your hair is light. You can wait to shave."

But when Clem asked Nora for a razor on her thirteenth birthday, her mother had sneered. Nora was a women's libber. She supported the Equal Rights Amendment and didn't believe in makeup, or bras, or shaving her body hair. So they compromised—Clem could wear a bra, but she didn't shave.

Coco had told her, "You can be a liberated woman without being all hairy. Just buy a Flicker like everybody else. You know, one of those new disposable razors?" But Clem and Nora had a deal, so Clem didn't shave.

She couldn't tell all that to Beth, though. She needed a good comeback, or Beth would probably tease her about leg hair again . . . and again.

"No, it's not the style in Cambridge," Clem said, "Not yet, anyway. But I'm doing my best to enlighten people."

"Ha. That's a good one," Beth said without smiling. "So,

Washashore, why are you here on the Island? Your parents some of those summer people who think it might be fun to come and live among the locals for a while? An educational-type experience?"

Clem felt like Beth had slapped her. Even during vacations, when she was a "summer person" rather than a year-round resident, Clem had always felt at home on the Vineyard. Like she belonged here. But Beth's words made her feel like she didn't belong anywhere.

"No story really," Clem answered.

"Then why did you come here?"

"Why does anybody move anywhere?" Clem looked around for a trash can to throw her bag in. "Because it seems like a nice place to live."

"That's what all the washashores say." Beth laughed. "Until it gets cold and the fancy restaurants where the summer people eat close for the winter. Where will you eat then? James Taylor and Carly Simon's house?"

"Oh, I'll probably just get my meals shipped in from Boston," Clem said. "Isn't that what everybody does?"

Clem spotted Sandy walking toward them. She always wore Gloria Vanderbilt jeans and heels—today she had on open-toed Candie's sandals. Her hair winged back on both sides of her face in a Farrah Fawcett flip. Back in Cambridge, Clem and Coco would giggle about the cheerleader types who dressed and wore their hair that way, but Sandy was nice. She'd been more friendly to Clem than anyone else at school.

"Hi guys!" she said brightly. "Did you all do the math homework?"

"Most of it," Clem answered.

Beth rolled her eyes, eased off the railing, and ambled away. "Birkenstocks and Candie's. What a combination!"

"Don't mind Beth." Sandy leaned in to whisper. "She's always like that. Her family's been on the Island like forever and she acts like she owns the place. But, you know, she has a hard time. Her dad's trucking business hasn't been doing so good. They had to sell a bunch of property."

"Really?"

Sandy nodded vigorously.

"How do you know all this?" Clem asked.

"Everybody does," she answered, pulling a Strawberry Lip Smacker out of her pocket. "It's a small island." She wiped the balm across her lips.

Clem thought about that. Then she asked, "What's a washashore?"

Sandy flushed. "Did Beth call you that?"

Clem nodded.

"Well, it's . . . not a compliment."

"I could tell."

Sandy slipped the Lip Smacker back in her pocket. "All it

really means is you didn't grow up here. You moved to the Vineyard from off-island. But, for some people, it means you don't belong. You're an outsider."

"I guess that's true enough," said Clem.

"Well, I don't think of you that way," said Sandy. "Hey—I like your shorts."

Clem had on her favorite Army surplus olive-drab cutoffs. Plus the rest of her usual uniform: Birkenstock sandals, a faded T-shirt (today she was wearing one that she and Adam had tie-dyed together), and a beaded choker. Sandy was obviously reaching. But that was nice, in a way.

"I got them at the Army-Navy store in Boston," she said. "Do you have one of those here?"

"Nope." Sandy looped her arm through Clem's as the bell rang and they turned toward the school. "But I can show you the best places to shop. Update your look a little."

Clem had to try hard not to smile. That was never going to happen. But she took Sandy's arm and kept the thought to herself.

After lunch, she had science. They were supposed to be reading the ecology chapter in their textbooks and filling out a worksheet while Jill, the teacher, walked around checking their work. Clem tried to concentrate, but she couldn't help looking around the room and thinking about Coco. How would she describe the boys here next time they talked?

There wasn't much to report, really. Certainly nobody Coco would find cute. But there was one boy who interested Clem a little. His name was Daniel. Beth called him "Bird Boy." Clem didn't know why. Maybe it was because he was thin and his legs were long. Clem had watched him fold them awkwardly under his desk. Like he was climbing into the back seat of a Ford Fiesta. He had fair skin, and his cheeks and the tip of his nose were rosy from sunburn. His bright blond hair flopped into his eyes and was shaggy in the back. He needed a haircut, Clem thought. On second thought, maybe not. She liked the way it looked.

Daniel wrote something on his paper and glanced up. Clem looked down at her book so he wouldn't catch her staring. Her face felt warm and she hoped he couldn't see she was blushing. His eyes were so blue. Frosty blue, like sea glass.

Jill stopped in front of Clem's desk. "What do you have down there?"

Clem looked up at the teacher. "Just my book. We're supposed to be reading, right?"

Jill smiled.

She was pretty, Clem thought, and young. She wore a wrap-around skirt and a peasant blouse. Her brown hair hung in a long braid down her back.

14

"No, I mean that." She pointed to Clem's book, tucked away beneath her seat. "What are you reading?"

Clem passed her the book—*Under the Sea-Wind*, by Rachel Carson. "My dad gave it to me."

"This book will change the way you look at the ocean," Adam had told her, tapping his finger on the book. "Look around you. Try to see the way this author sees."

"Nice gift," said Jill. "Rachel Carson is one of my absolute favorite authors. Are you enjoying it?"

"I'm not very far along," Clem answered.

"Oh, I hope you like it. It's perfect for this unit. And her writing is like poetry."

Beth, a few seats away, coughed loudly.

"Okay," Clem said. She agreed with Jill, although she didn't want to say it in front of everybody, especially Beth. Rachel Carson had words for things Clem didn't even know had names. Sea wrack. Panicles. Ghost crabs. Marsh samphire. Comb jellies. She had started a list, wondering how many of these birds and creatures and plants she could find on Martha's Vineyard.

Jill handed her back the book.

At the end of the day, Beth elbowed Clem on the way out the door.

"Teacher's pet," she muttered.

Nora was in the kitchen waiting when Clem got home from school. She was wearing bell-bottom jeans, cinched around her narrow hips with a fringed macramé belt that Clem had made for her in fifth grade. She gave her mother a hug, and was surprised at how thin she felt. Nora barely seemed to eat these days.

Nora took a step back, still holding Clem's shoulders. "You survived!"

"Of course I did!" Clem patted her mother's hand.

"Go on, sit down." Nora pulled out a chair. "I want to hear about your day."

A snack was spread on the table like a feast, Nora-style: whole wheat bread, an apple, a knife, and a jar of crunchy peanut butter from the natural foods store. Next to the peanut butter was a letter.

It was from Adam, Clem could tell, and it was addressed to her. She reached for the letter and started to open it, then changed her mind and slipped it into her pocket. She wanted to read it in private. Then she saw Nora watching her.

"You can read it after me," she said.

"Oh, no," said Nora. "It's your letter." She went to the cabinet and took out a plate. "How was your day?"

"It was fine," Clem answered.

"Just fine?"

"Yup." Clem dug the knife into the peanut butter. "Pretty quiet."

"That's good." Nora put the plate in front of Clem. "What about school? Was that fine?"

"Yup.

"So . . . what are you doing in math?"

Clem's mind went blank. Variables. Solve for x. "Um, algebra?"

"Well, of course algebra. Do you have the book?"

"No, I don't think so. I don't need . . ."

"Please bring it home tomorrow so I can take a look."

"Okay." Clem took a bite of the sandwich. Thick peanut butter stuck in her throat. She didn't like being interrogated.

"How about English? Did you get a syllabus?"

Clem didn't know what a syllabus was. Why didn't her mother just ask the school these questions? Irritated, she reached into her pack and pulled out the textbook. "Here. You can see for yourself."

"No need to get snippy," said Nora. "You're a gifted student, and you can't afford to waste a year of your education."

"What makes you think I would?" Clem put down her sandwich and stood up.

"You just don't sound very . . . engaged."

"What do you expect? It's the second week of school!"

Clem said. "Besides, it wasn't my idea to come here. If you have a problem with the school, you should have thought of that before we left Boston!"

"It's not the school I'm having a problem with!" Nora grabbed the plate and knife and dumped them in the sink.

Clem stood still, staring at Nora. Then she turned and went out, letting the screen door slam behind her.

3

Sunshine Girl

Clem shot down the hill on her ten-speed bike, away from the cottage.

She hit the bottom and pedaled hard past the art gallery and the tourist shops, the fish markets, the public shower, and the gas station. She sped to the end of the road and into a parking lot. Panting, Clem hopped off her bike.

On her left was the long stone wall of the breakwater and a row of private yachts and power boats tied to a pier. Menemsha Beach lay straight ahead, just beyond the parking lot. She locked her bike, slipped off her sandals, and walked quickly onto the sand.

Clem had been coming to Menemsha her entire life and she knew the beach by heart: the pebbly sand on the soles of her feet, the dangerous jagged rocks hidden beneath the surf, and the way the water looked in all kinds of weather. She knew this place the way she knew the feel of Adam's hand on her forehead when he used to tuck her in at night. Or the scent of Nora's patchouli perfume when she gave Clem a hug. She wanted to wrap herself in the beach like a tattered and beloved blanket.

This was her favorite kind of day—not yet cold, but gray and blustery. The wind made her T-shirt into a sail and whipped her hair into sharp strings that slapped her face. Clem turned and headed up the beach, away from the parking lot.

She walked and walked, and then turned toward the waves and breathed deeply, tasting the tang of the sea. The tight knot of anger and dismay in her chest slowly loosened. Nora, school, Beth—they all slipped away.

Except for . . . Adam.

Clem still had his letter in her pocket. She remembered the hungry and hurt look on Nora's face when she tucked the letter away. She wondered if Nora got letters from Adam. Maybe she didn't. Clem felt a little guilty for wanting to keep Adam's letter to herself.

She sat on a boulder and carefully slid the single sheet of paper out of the envelope. She recognized Adam's typing right away because his old typewriter printed every "e" out of line with the rest of the letters. He punched the periods so hard that they sometimes made a tiny hole in the paper. The thin typing paper rattled in the wind and she gripped it with both hands.

Dear Clem,

How's my favorite Sunshine Girl? I'm sorry it's been so long since my last letter; your old man is a useless correspondent. The days just blend one into another and suddenly I see a month has passed . . .

Things are good here. I've finally learned to fend for myself on the feeding front—cooking was never a problem but keeping the refrigerator stocked is a new skill for me. And I'm even getting a little writing done. Who knew that Ohio would be the place where I would get my poetry mojo back? I don't know if they're any good, but I've got at least six new poems in a folder on my desk. Are you proud of me?

I hope the Island is treating you and Nora well. I miss it terribly, especially the water, which is in short supply here in landlocked Columbus. Please give my regards to the man behind the counter at Seward's Market, and to the gulls at Lucy Vincent Beach . . .

Adam wrote a whole paragraph about the classes he would be teaching this quarter. Clem tried to picture Adam's face and hear his voice in her head, but it was hard. She hadn't seen him in almost four months.

At the bottom, he'd scrawled *xoxo Adam* and *P.S. Give your mother a hug for me and don't forget to dead-head the rhododendrons so they bloom again next summer. I love you.*

Clem read the letter twice. Somehow she felt cheated. This letter didn't make her feel any closer to him. Why didn't Adam write that he missed her? Or tell her when she would see him? Or ask her questions about her life?

She stood and put the letter back in her pocket, then began walking again. A gull glided past, skimming low over the water, and she realized that the beach was alive with birds. She stopped to watch.

There was another gull, stalking along the sand, and a third on the water, bobbing in the waves. Long-beaked sandpipers scampered in a group near the water's edge. Black-and-white terns wobbled in the air, fighting the wind.

High above, a bird traced lazy circles in the sky. It flew slowly, stopping occasionally to hover and drop down a notch, as if to get a better look at something in the water below. It was a big bird, white underneath, with brown-and-white striped feathers and dark brown patches at the bend in its wings. At its wingtips, long feathers spread out like fingers.

The bird suddenly dropped toward the ocean. So fast that Clem gasped. Wings tucked, it fell like a stone. Just before it hit the water, the bird spread its wings and lifted its head, stretching its feet toward the waves.

With a giant splash, the big bird hit the waves and plunged underwater.

One . . . two . . . three . . . Clem counted silently.

The bird burst out of the water, flapping madly. Water droplets flew everywhere. The bird rose back into the air, claws clamped around a struggling fish.

In the book Adam had given her, there was a bird that fished just that way. Rachel Carson called the bird *Pandion*. He dropped from the sky to catch a fish, then an eagle stole it from him.

The bird flew off and Clem turned and headed farther up the beach. She walked until she reached the sign marked END OF PUBLIC BEACH.

Then, just ahead, she saw something dark in the foamy water where the waves broke on the sand.

So many things washed onto the beach: lobster traps and chunks of buoys and tangled bits of net, wooden planks and coils of nylon rope, TAB cans, old tires, watermelon rinds, wine bottles and tampon applicators, logs and roots and branches worn smooth by the waves. Maybe it was driftwood, silvery and gnarled. She would take it back to the cottage to put on the mantel, if she could manage it on her bike.

But as she got closer, Clem saw it was a floppy, bedraggled thing. A large wave pushed it all the way up onto the beach.

It was a bird.

Clem could tell right away that the bird was dead. It lay on its back, wings outstretched, the long wing feathers fanned out on the sand. It was huge. Instinctively, Clem bent over the bird and spread her arms, mirroring its pose. Its wingspan had to be about five feet, almost as wide as her own.

The bird's wings were striped with brown and white—just like the bird she had seen fishing. Maybe they were the same kind. This bird's neck, though, bent awkwardly and its head lolled to one side. Its short, hooked beak and flared nostrils gave it a scornful look. One yellow eye, circled in black, seemed to stare up at her. Its curved talons, long as hawthorns, were clenched in a deadly-looking grip. But its legs folded uselessly against its body.

Clem crouched down and gently touched the bird's soft, white breast. The wet feathers felt cold but silky smooth. She wasn't disgusted. Instead, Clem felt her heart go out to the bird. It was beautiful and strong, even in death.

That's when she noticed the bands. On the bird's left leg was a tight metal band, engraved with numbers. On its right were two colored plastic bracelets—one orange, one green. Why were they there? How had anyone gotten close enough to this huge wild sea bird to place bands on its legs?

Feeling curious, she grasped one of the bird's legs. It was scaly and thick. She ran a finger along a smooth, sharp talon. Without thinking, she pulled her jackknife out of her pocket and cut off the bands. The plastic ones sliced right off and dropped to the sand. To get the metal one off, Clem had to stick the tip of her blade under the band and twist and pry until it bent open.

She picked up the bands and stood, looked around quickly, and stuck them in the pocket of her shorts.

4

Birds of North America

The following Tuesday night, Clem was waiting in the kitchen when the phone rang at eight thirty. She answered after one ring. Nora was away in Boston again, and this week Adam was calling to check up on her.

"Adam?"

"Sunshine! What's shakin'?"

Clem smiled as she carried the phone across the room and settled on the sofa. Sunshine was Adam's special corny nickname for her. He got it from the TV ad where a mom serves her kids breakfast, looks at the camera, and says: "A day without orange juice is like a day without sunshine." Adam thought the ad was hilarious and, since a clementine is a small orange, he started calling her Sunshine. The name stuck.

"Just finishing my homework. I have to memorize all the prepositions. Aboard, about, above, across . . ."

"After, against, along, among, around, at," he finished, chuckling. "I'm glad to know the old parts of speech haven't gone out of style. You never know when a preposition will come in handy."

"Except why would you need to be able to list them?" Clem asked. "Has that special knowledge ever come in handy for you?"

"Never. At least, not until now."

Adam liked to say that school was important, but life was more so. Sometimes he picked Clem up early from school so they could prowl the secondhand bookstores in Harvard Square. Every year, on the first warm day in May, Adam let her skip school. The two of them would drive to the beach at Plum Island in his Karmann Ghia two-seater with the top down. Last spring, he let her stand up while he drove. She remembered gripping the windshield tight as the sea breeze washed her face.

Nora didn't come. She thought school should take priority. But she never stopped them, either.

"Have your fall classes started yet?" Clem asked. "You were on break last time you wrote me."

"Yep, started on Tuesday. This group is just as sharp as the last one. I don't know what I expected Midwestern kids to be like—placid and complacent, maybe—but I was way off. They're a little conservative for my taste, but they're inquisitive.

We're getting some good discussions going." He sounded happy and upbeat.

Clem felt a pang of jealousy. His new students got to be with the Adam she missed. The Adam who used to make her smoothies after school and sit with her on the porch of their second-floor apartment, talking nonsense.

"Tut, tut, it looks like rain," he might say on a bright, clear day, quoting from her old favorite, *Winnie-the-Pooh*.

Or he'd smile and quote "Jabberwocky" from *Alice Through the Looking-Glass*: "Have you been out grabing with the mome raths on this brillig day?"

She would answer with, "I'm feeling a little mimsy," or something equally nerdy. They had their own secret code. Nerdy or not, Clem liked it. And she missed it.

"What about the other professors? Are they nice?" she asked.

"There are a couple of pretty decent poets on the faculty, and an editor at the university press has already approached me about a book. I'm having dinner with her tonight, actually."

"At a restaurant?" Clem's voice squeaked a little. Nora and Adam almost never ate out. It was too expensive. The idea of Adam having dinner out with a woman who wasn't Nora made Clem feel queasy.

"Yup. A little Italian joint." Adam paused.

Clem could tell he guessed what she was thinking.

"It's a working dinner, Clem. Strictly professional," he said.

"To talk about the book?"

"Yes."

"Oh." Clem stood up, holding the phone in one hand and the receiver in the other, and began to pace. "When are you going to visit?"

"Oh, honey, I miss you and Nora terribly but I can't possibly get back to Boston before Thanksgiving. There just isn't time to drive, and I can't afford to fly."

"Then could I come see you?"

"That would cost just as much. Plus, you wouldn't believe how small this apartment is. There really isn't any place for you to sleep."

Clem had slept on the floor a zillion times. She stopped near the window and looked out, but it was dark outside and the room was bright. All she could see was her own reflection.

"Are you doing okay with all the changes?" Adam asked. "It's a lot, I know. New school, new place, new kids. How are things going?"

For a moment, Clem considered telling Adam everything—how much she missed him and their city apartment and Coco, how strange and different she felt at school, how thin and jumpy Nora had become. The truth was, she wished they were all still together in Boston.

But what would be the point of telling him all that? Nothing would change.

"I'm great," she said.

"That's good." Adam sounded relieved. "And Nora? How's your mother doing?"

"She's all right, I guess," Clem answered, trying to sound cheerful. "But shouldn't you ask her that?" His question made Clem feel awkward. Like telling Adam any more would be talking behind Nora's back.

"Oh." Adam sounded surprised. "I guess I was hoping for your perspective."

"She's working a lot, like always," said Clem. That much was true.

"That makes two of us, then."

There was a pause, and Clem felt Adam about to end the call. He took a breath. "Well—"

"Wait!" Clem cut him off. "I almost forgot—you know that book you used to use to look up birds?"

"My Golden Field Guide? *Birds of North America*? Wow. I love that book. I haven't thought about it in ages."

"Can you send it to me?"

"The book?"

"Yes. I need it."

"You know, I don't have it," Adam said. "Actually, I think it's there."

"Here?"

"Yes—right there in the cottage. Look on the shelf in the kitchen," he said. "With Nana's cookbooks."

Clem put the receiver down and ran to the kitchen. She used a chair to climb onto the counter so she could reach the shelf. She saw the book right away.

"Got it!" she shouted, although he probably couldn't hear.

She stepped back onto the chair. It wobbled and started to tip. At the last second she jumped off, smacking her forehead on the corner of a cabinet door she'd left open. She landed on her feet, still clutching the book. The chair fell, hitting the kitchen floor with a loud crack.

Clem touched her forehead, then looked at her fingertips.

Blood.

She went back into the living room, where Adam's voice was trickling from the phone that lay on the table. He sounded small and far away. Clem picked up the receiver.

"What's going on?" Adam asked.

"Sorry, a chair fell over. I had to get the book. I bumped my head."

"Are you all right?"

Clem wiped her hand across her throbbing forehead and looked at her fingers again. Less blood this time. Just a smear.

"Yeah, it's fine. What were you saying?"

"I want to know if you're okay with spending so much time alone."

Clem paused. Maybe she should tell Adam that she'd just nearly killed herself climbing on a chair and she had no idea what she would have done or who she would have called if something bad happened. She wondered what he would say about that. Would he drop everything and come home?

She knew the answer was no. There was nothing he could do, so there was no point in complaining.

"I'm fine." Clem pressed a paper napkin to her forehead. "Maybe I should write a book: *My Side of the Island.* Courageous girl survives on her own in the wilds of Martha's Vineyard. Nothing stands between her and the elements. The only thing is, there are all these tourists there . . ."

Adam laughed. Clem smiled. She could still make her dad laugh.

After putting a Band-Aid on her forehead, Clem sat down at the kitchen table with *Birds of North America.* She switched on the table lamp to see better, then brushed a cobweb from the edge of the pages and brought the book to her face. It smelled like moss and damp earth. Everything they left in this house through the winter got mildewy. She rifled through the book until she found the section on waterfowl. Turning the rippled pages slowly, she scanned for a picture of a bird like the one that had washed up on the beach.

The pages on the left side had descriptions of the birds and colored maps that showed where they lived. The right-side pages were crowded with drawings of birds perched on branches or flying. So many varieties! She marveled at how different they were in size and color and shape—and yet the same, as well, with their feathers and their wings and beaks. Clem found her bird on page 76, just beneath the bald eagle. She recognized the stripes on the wing and tail, the light belly, and the dark markings around its eyes, like goggles.

"It's an osprey!" she said out loud to the empty kitchen.

On the facing page was a description. "Osprey (Pandion haliaetus)."

Pandion. Just like in *Under the Sea-Wind*. That was an osprey, too.

"Uncommon; along seacoasts, lakes and rivers . . . Conspicuous crook in long wings and black wrist mark confirm identification of adults and young at great distance. Plumage is dark above, white below . . . While hunting, the birds hover, 50' to 150' high, then suddenly plunge, sometimes going completely under the water."

Just like the bird she'd seen catch the fish at Menemsha Beach.

So the flying bird and the dead bird were both ospreys. She looked back at the drawings. The osprey in the book had a glistening yellow eye. The dead bird's eye had been cloudy, she recalled, but just as yellow.

Clem got up and went to her room, taking the book with her. Every night, she emptied her pockets onto the top of the dresser. The bird's bands were still there, in a jumble of other items. She picked up the metal one and turned it over in her hand. It was incredibly light. A bunch of random letters and numbers were written on the band. Above them, in smaller letters, were the words "AVISE BIRD BAND WASH DC." Were you supposed to tell someone if you found a bird with a band like this? Maybe "avise" meant "advise." But as far as an address, "Wash DC" was pretty unspecific.

She turned to the back of the book to see if there was anything at the end or in the index about bird bands. Nothing. Clem felt like she needed to do something with the bands. But she didn't know what.

She got a baggie from the kitchen and put the bands into it and knotted the bag. Then she went back to her bedroom. She put the bag on her dresser with the jumble of other items from her pockets. Sea glass, ponytail holders, earrings, smooth stones, pencil stubs. Bird bands.

5

Bird Boy

Clem climbed up the school bus stairs and stopped, looking for a seat.

The bus was packed with ninth graders for the science class field trip today. Clem had never ridden a bus before this year. She could tell there were unwritten rules about who sits where, but she hadn't figured them out yet.

A sweatshirt flew through the air, then a lunch bag. Boys hopped from seat to seat while girls scrunched against the windows. Beth and her friends had taken over the back three rows with their feet up on the seats.

Clem took an empty seat about halfway back and looked out the window, feeling awkward. She was relieved when Sandy plopped down next to her.

"These boys are *so* immature, don't you think?" Sandy said. A Charleston Chew whizzed between their heads. She whipped around. "Hey! Didn't you hear? We're going to *Bird* World, not *Monkey* World!"

Sandy turned back to Clem. "How's it going? Everybody treating you right here?"

"Yeah, it's fine." Clem shrugged.

"But . . . ?"

"But nothing."

"Let me guess. Beth is a total bully and most of the other kids have no idea what to say to you because you're not from here and they haven't had fourteen years to get used to your face."

"Well, yeah, kinda. But it's all right."

"You want me to talk to somebody?"

"No, no, really, it's fine."

"Okay." Sandy smoothed the wings of hair on both sides of her head with a flick of her wrist—first the right side, then the left. "I guess you're the type who likes to handle stuff on your own."

Clem *was* the type who liked to handle stuff on her own. Well, not necessarily *liked*, but it was her way. "Have you been to this place before?" she asked. "Bird World?"

"Oh, yeah, we go every year. Crazy guy who runs it actually lives there! But he's nice, though." Sandy leaned in and lowered her voice. "I think Jill and he might be a couple. I saw them together once at Cronig's Market. Personally, I don't see it."

Clem hadn't given any thought to their teacher's private life. It was interesting to consider.

"Hey, SANDY!"

A sneaker came flying through the air and landed in her lap. Sandy jumped up, hair whirling, and stared at a boy named Joe.

He threw back his head and laughed, his face flushed.

"Why, you . . . ," Sandy sputtered.

She sounded furious, but Clem could tell she wasn't. She was fake furious.

"Oh my God, what a spaz. Excuse me," Sandy said. "We'll talk more later."

She walked back a few rows and plunked down in the seat next to Joe. The bus engine started up and they rolled out of the parking lot. Clem went back to looking out the window.

Bird World was at the end of a long dirt driveway in a town called Gay Head at the western tip of Martha's Vineyard. The bus lumbered to a stop in front of a simple one-story house in a clearing in the woods. Clem saw clusters of cages scattered about the property. Some were smallish, like rabbit hutches. Others were as big as trailers.

Before anyone got up, a man came bounding up the steps of the bus.

"Howdy," he said. "I'm Bo Jameson. Welcome to my

home. Come on out and meet the family. I'm gonna ask you to be kinda quiet, though, so you don't wake the babies." He chuckled. "Baby birds, that is."

Bo was medium height and a little stocky. His thick hair was combed straight back and his face was creased with deep lines. He had crinkles around his eyes, like he squinted a lot in the sun. Clem thought he looked nice, and she disagreed with Sandy. She could definitely imagine him with their pretty, outdoorsy science teacher.

"Look all you want, but don't go poking anything into the cages—especially your fingers—and show some respect for the animals. I'll meet you all right in front of the house in about twenty minutes."

Clem got off the bus. She noticed Sandy and Joe disappearing together behind one of the trailer-sized cages. It made her think of boy-crazy Coco. She smiled.

In front of the house, a flock of white ducks milled around the patchy lawn like grownups at a cocktail party. One boy crouched down and sprinted directly into the gaggle of birds, causing them to scatter, beating their wings and clacking.

Clem wondered how Bo would react—maybe he would order them all back on the bus. But he just sauntered over to the boy and his friends and said something that made them laugh, then gently herded them toward the larger cages. Clem liked that.

She went the other way, toward the small cages. The wooden cages were stacked like mailboxes at the post office. They had no bars or mesh—only a round opening in the front. Clem wondered what kind of birds used the boxes, and if they went in and out whenever they liked.

"It looks inviting, doesn't it?" said a voice just behind her right shoulder. "But I think it's vacant. The purple martins have all gone south for the winter."

Clem turned. Daniel stood a few feet away. The one the kids called Bird Boy. Standing so close, he seemed even taller than she'd thought. She had to tip her head back to meet his eyes.

"You shouldn't sneak up on people!" Her face felt hot.

"I'm sorry. I didn't mean to startle you." He gazed down at her with a solemn expression, then took a step back.

Clem shook her head. "It's okay."

He took another step back and started to turn away.

"Wait!" said Clem.

He turned back toward her.

"What are purple martins?"

"They are a species of songbird," he answered. "People often build nesting houses to attract them because they like to eat mosquitoes," he said. "They are nice birds to have around." His voice was calm and even, and he seemed to choose each word deliberately.

Clem remembered the descriptions in *Birds of North America*. Each species had a different song. "What do purple martins sound like?"

"Like an opera of chattering," he said, then looked down at the ground, as if embarrassed by his words.

Clem studied Daniel. It was easier to look at him when he didn't have those blue eyes fixed on her. She liked his odd, specific words. Kind of like Rachel Carson's.

And in an odd, specific way, he was beautiful.

Across the yard, Jill raised her hand high. "Gather around, everyone!"

Clem started over, expecting Daniel would walk with her. But he dropped behind and when she turned to say something to him, he was gone. Clem found a mossy spot and sat down. She forced herself not to look around for him.

"Students, Bo has some information to share with you," said Jill.

She sat down on the ground. Bo stood in front of the group. He was wearing a long pair of thick leather gloves. He disappeared into one of the large cages. In a moment, he came out.

He had an osprey in his arms.

With its wings folded, the bird didn't look so big. But then Bo offered the bird his gloved hand and it stepped on, gripping the leather with dangerous-looking talons. The osprey spread its long wings and flapped them gently. Clem felt the air stir.

"Whoa," someone exclaimed, and the students giggled nervously. Those in front edged away and those in back tried to get a better view. Bo slowly moved his arm to the side. The osprey folded its wings and took a proud stance, chest out. It turned its head to the side and fixed one bright yellow eye on the students.

Clem stared back, fascinated by the bird's fierceness.

Then she noticed the bands on its legs. One metal, one plastic. Just like the ones in the baggie on her dresser.

"You all know this bird, right? She's an osprey. Some call her a fish hawk. Isn't she a beauty? Her name is Wendy. Like in *Peter Pan*. The girl who flew through the air and survived when one of the boys in Neverland shot her down with an arrow.

"She's my little darlin', and there's not too many like her in captivity." Bo looked at the bird fondly. "Not too many wild any more, either. Not too many at all."

"I bet she's worth a lot of money!" someone yelled.

"Yeah," said Beth. "Stuffed!"

"Does she always stay in that cage?" asked one of the girls. "Doesn't she want to be free?"

Bo smiled. "Well, she doesn't love it, that's for sure. But she might not be able to take care of herself if I let her go. She was shot in the wing by a hunter and it never healed right. She's better off here. I take her out and let her fly a couple of times a week. She can't go high like the others or fly for very long, but still, it's a grand thing to see."

A dozen hands went up. Bo answered each question patiently. What did the bird eat? (Only fish.) How old was she? (He had no idea, but ospreys could live as long as thirty years.) Was she dangerous? (Yes, if you weren't careful.)

Clem hadn't spoken much in class so far. She'd always been quiet in school—and more so when she didn't know people. But she was so curious. She raised her hand and Bo pointed to her.

"How can ospreys fish from so high up?"

"Ah," said Bo. "That's the million dollar question. Didja see'em fishing?"

"Once," Clem answered.

"Quite a sight, isn't it?"

Clem squirmed a little. Everyone was looking at her. "I just think it's amazing how they can see the fish from so far up, then grab them with their feet. Fish are so quick."

"You're right. Fish are quick. But ospreys got specially constructed eyes that let them see real good—much better than we do. And you see the dark circles around her eyes? Those are for the glare, so she can see fish underwater—like she was wearin' Ray-Bans. An osprey can see a fish in the water from 130 feet up in the air. And look at these feet."

Bo held the bird in front of him, gripping her by the wings, then held up one of her feet. It looked just like the feet Clem had touched on the beach. Strong and white, with scaly skin— and deadly-looking curved black talons.

"She's got tiny scales on the bottom of these toes like sharp hooks that let her grip the fish," said Bo. "And see how that big toe points backward? It's reversible. That gives her a better hold.

"And man, are they fast. An osprey can snap its claws shut on a fish in two one-thousandths of a second." He chuckled. "I guess somebody timed it. They dive in the water feet first, and their nostrils close up to keep the water out.

"Scientists call these here birds a miracle of adaptation."

Clem raised her hand again. "You said there weren't many left. Are they dying out?"

Bo frowned. "Well, they were." His eyes traveled over the group. "You want to tell them what's been killing these birds, Daniel?"

The group murmured and everybody turned to follow Bo's glance. Daniel was standing at the back, leaning against a tree. He suddenly looked uncomfortable.

"DDT," he said.

"That's right," said Bo. "DDT. Nasty stuff. It was the strongest poison ever used for insect control, and they used to spray it all over the place to fight mosquitoes. But it killed a lot more than mosquitoes."

Jill got to her feet. "There's a book that tells the whole story about how that happened. It's called *Silent Spring*. By Rachel Carson. I have it back at school and will be happy to share it with anyone who is interested." She looked straight at Clem.

Rachel Carson. The author of *Under the Sea-Wind*, the book Adam had given her.

"Because of that book, DDT was banned a few years back," Jill went on. "Here on the Vineyard, Bo and some others are trying to bring the ospreys back. But it's not easy. There are other obstacles, like where to build nests. Ospreys are particular about where they nest. With all the building going on, there are fewer and fewer places for them to raise families."

Bo nodded. He looked at Jill with an admiring expression.

She continued. "Bo has put up nesting platforms for the ospreys all over the Vineyard. Later this fall, we're going to go out to a site and take a look at one of them. If I can get the school to sign off on it, we're going to help put up a nesting pole, too."

Beth's hand shot up.

"You know, not everybody thinks those poles are a good thing," she said. "They're ugly. Block people's view. Mess up the beach."

Bo tilted his head a little to the side and looked at Beth thoughtfully.

"You know, that's an interesting point, Beth." said Jill. "I think it's a good topic for discussion. We'll talk about it when we do our site visit."

Bo brought out several more birds: an owl, a cormorant, a ring-necked pheasant. He explained that people brought him wild birds that were sick or wounded and he nursed them back to health.

Clem was only half paying attention. She was wondering about her bird. Was it killed by DDT?

Back on the bus, Clem took a window seat and looked back at Bird World. Bo walked out of Wendy's cage and closed the door. Daniel stood next to him, holding the padlock. He slipped it through the hasp, clicked it shut and spun the dial. Like he'd done it a thousand times before. Bo put a hand on Daniel's shoulder and said something. Then Daniel ran to the bus.

The seat next to Clem was open. She hoped he would sit there, but she didn't want to draw attention to herself by calling his name. Daniel found an empty seat near the front of the bus and Clem wished she felt braver. She wanted to talk to him again. And not only because he seemed to know about birds.

6

You Haven't Seen Her Lately

That night, Clem was nearly asleep when she heard Nora's voice in the kitchen. Her mother was on the phone.

"That's ridiculous," Nora said. "How can you expect us to do that?"

Clem knew that tone. She was talking to Adam.

"It's not possible. You know how Addison would take it if I asked for a leave at this point. I might as well kiss this job good-bye."

She was talking about her job. Addison was the chairperson of the anthropology department at the university. Kind of like Nora's boss.

There was a long silence. That meant her father was talking.

"Really, Adam?" said Nora. "I can't believe you're even suggesting it!"

Her mother lowered her voice and started whispering.

Clem got out of bed and moved closer to the door. But she couldn't hear anything. After a few minutes, Clem heard a clack as Nora returned the phone to its cradle. Then she heard her mother's bedroom door shut.

Clem got back in bed but she tossed restlessly for a long time before drifting off to sleep.

When Clem walked into the kitchen the next morning, Nora was already sitting at the table with a cup of coffee. She looked tired.

Clem reached up into the cabinet for a box of cereal. "Were you talking to Adam last night?"

"Yes. Did I wake you?"

"Maybe. I guess I went right back to sleep." Clem turned away quickly and poured a bowl of puffed rice. "What were you guys talking about?"

Nora sighed. "He wants us to move to Ohio."

"Really?" Clem had only thought about Adam coming home, not them going to him. "Maybe that would be okay."

Nora looked grim. "He knows it's impossible."

"Why?" asked Clem, raising her voice. "Why do we have to live out here with him so far away? It doesn't make sense! I miss him!"

"Clementine, I know this is hard . . ."

"You don't know anything!" Clem grabbed her bowl of dry cereal and dumped it in the trash. Nora raised her eyebrows and Clem felt a little embarrassed at her childish gesture.

"Listen, Clementine. Do you think this is all *my* fault? Do you think I just up and decided to move out here with you for my own fun and amusement?"

"How should I know?"

"I think you know." Nora stood up from the table. "Let me ask you this. Who is the one who lost his job? Who is the one whose poetic *muse* "—her voice trembled—"is more important than his paycheck? Who moved to Ohio?" Nora's eyes glittered angrily.

Clem was shocked. How could Nora be so mad at Adam? He was so . . . lovable!

When her parents fought at home, Nora usually got all icy and quiet. Then Adam would put his arms around her and say sweet things to charm her back into a good humor. He could coax a smile out of her pretty quickly. But Adam wasn't here to make things right.

"He *had* to go to Ohio, didn't he?" said Clem. "It was the only job he could get!"

"Yes, but did you ever wonder why?" Nora asked. "Why wouldn't anybody on the East Coast hire him, when he's such a talented poet?"

"I don't know. Why?" Clem felt a tear slip down her cheek.

48

Nora shouldn't talk about Adam this way. She was supposed to be on his side. It scared her to hear the venom in her mother's voice. She brushed the tear away with her sleeve.

Nora suddenly looked concerned.

"Oh, honey. I didn't mean your father did something bad. But he's so unrealistic. He's a wonderful poet, but that's not enough. He needs to grow up—go to committee meetings— get *along* with people. He needs to be serious."

Nora picked up her coffee cup and carried it to the sink. She returned to the table and began stacking her scattered papers and folders.

"I know it's hard for you to understand, Clementine. You want us all to be together. We want that, too, but we haven't figured out the logistics. We're trying, I promise."

"I know," said Clem. But she really wasn't sure.

Nora glanced at the clock. "Time to get going. You'll miss the bus."

That evening Nora went to Cronig's for groceries and Clem called Coco.

"Island Girl! What's up? You don't usually call me on Thursdays!"

"I just—I guess I just need to talk."

"What's wrong?"

"Nothing, really. But Coco—your parents fight sometimes, don't they?"

"Oh my God, Clem, they fight all the time. All. The. Time! It's like, if they're not bickering about something, I better go check their pulses."

"But they make up?"

"I don't know—they don't really need to. Fighting is like breathing to them. My mom's got that Cuban temper, you know? At least that's what my dad says. And he is so stubborn. Fighting is just what they do. What's going on?"

"I heard Nora talking to Adam on the phone. She was really mad. He wants us to move to Ohio."

"No way—I would *never* see you!"

"We're not going, Coco. But I think he might stay in Ohio."

"You think they're splitting up? Really?"

"I don't know, Coco." Clem paused. "Maybe Adam went to Ohio to get away from Nora."

"Why would he do that? Your mom is great!"

Clem slid her back down the wall until she was sitting on the floor. "You haven't seen her lately."

"What do you mean?"

These days, Nora seemed sad and tired. She got mad all the time. And she barely ate. When Clem packed Nora's lunch for the trips to Boston, she always tried to put in lots of nourishing food. Boiled eggs. Hunks of cheese. Homemade oatmeal cookies. Like if she could just fatten her mother up, things would be better.

"Clem?"

"Coco, I don't know if I can explain it," she said. When Coco's parents fought, it was nothing like Adam and Nora. They just yelled a lot, then made up. It was silly to even try to compare.

"*Try* to explain," said Coco.

"I just . . . I think I want to talk about something else."

Coco let out an exasperated sigh. "Listen, Island Girl, stop worrying. You've got the coolest parents anyone could have. So romantic. Hippie college kids who fell in love and had a baby and got married. And take it from me—a little fighting is a good thing. It keeps a marriage spicy."

"Spicy?"

"Yeah, spicy. Sexy!"

"Ew, Coco, I don't want to think about that!"

"My parents can't wait to go upstairs after a good fight."

"Okay, enough about that."

"You should stop worrying. You know what they say: Absence makes the heart grow fonder."

"Then I'll try to stop thinking about it. I'm sure it's nothing."

"Definitely nothing."

"Thanks, Coco. Good night, John-Boy."

"G'night, Mary Ellen."

She hung up the phone. For the first time ever, talking to Coco hadn't made Clem feel the slightest bit better.

7

More About the Ospreys

Clem reached the top of the steep hill and hopped off her bike. Sucking in gulps of air, she peeled her moist T-shirt away from her stomach. The Indian summer sun felt hot on her face, a welcome sensation on this Saturday in late October.

From this spot, Clem could see almost all of Menemsha Pond. A pair of sailboats made their way slowly across. In summer, the blue water of the big salt pond would be speckled with sails—the little striped isosceles triangles of Sunfishes and the taller sails of the catboats. Clem imagined holding tight to the tiller of a Laser, steering the boat and feeling the cool wind on her skin.

"*Yee-ow, yo, yo, yo.*"

Clem looked up to see a herring gull soaring overhead. She slipped her hand into her pocket and fingered the little bag that held the bands. Still there.

Feeling cooler, Clem climbed back on her bike and coasted down the hill. It was about eight miles from her house to Bird World. Almost an hour's ride. She had biked from her house to the Menemsha Crossroad, past the little general store and real estate office at Beetlebung Corner. Now she pedaled hard over five miles of hilly, winding road all the way out to the tip of the Island and turned right just before the lighthouse and the Gay Head tourist trap.

That was where they sold rubber tomahawks and little plastic Indian dolls with soft black hair and fake-leather dresses and eyes that closed when you tilted them back. Nora and Adam bought her one when she was about four. She must have begged for it, because it was not the kind of toy they usually got her. They chose wooden, handmade, "educational" toys. But Clem loved that doll. She thought her Indian girl was the most glamorous doll in the world.

Thinking about the doll reminded her of her argument with Nora. She speeded up, trying to ride it out of her mind.

Finally, breathing hard, Clem turned onto the dirt drive leading to Bird World. As she approached the building, her heart sank. The place looked deserted. No pickup truck in the driveway, no sign of Bo. She rode up to the house. The sign on the door read: "Open MWFS 9 to 12."

She checked her watch. It was one o'clock.

Rats. Clem leaned her bike against a tree and walked over to

Wendy's cage. The osprey sat on her perch at the far end of the cage with her head turned to the side. She was so still, she could have been a statue.

Clem walked around to the side of the cage for a closer view. Now she could see the curved, pointy beak and the long claws curled around the perch. Clem imagined that sharp beak tearing into a fish. Wendy turned and looked at Clem straight on, and it seemed almost as if she was frowning. Clem felt a pang of sadness for the powerful bird, locked in a cage.

"Do you miss that life?" Clem asked aloud. "Diving for fish and soaring in the sky?"

Of course, Clem remembered, without Bo's help, Wendy would have died after she was shot. Living in this cage kept her safe.

Clem turned to leave. She would come back next week.

Just then, Bo's pickup truck bumped into view, rattling over the rutted road. It stopped in the turnaround and Bo emerged, frowning.

"Can I help you?"

"I—I'm sorry. I didn't know you were closed."

The frown relaxed. "You came to see the animals?"

"Well, I . . ."

Bo smiled. "Wait. I remember you. You were here with Jill's school group, right?"

Clem nodded.

"You asked about the ospreys."

She nodded again.

"Name?"

"Clementine Harper."

"Where'd ya ride from?"

"Near Menemsha."

"That's a pretty good ride. I think I've got some lemonade in the fridge."

Bo's kitchen was tidy and small. A coffeemaker sat on the counter with two mugs next to it. A bulletin board covered with photos hung over a green Formica table. Clem saw a photo of Bo crouching in the back of a canoe, gripping binoculars. A woman sat in the bow, her back to the camera. Clem stepped closer to the bulletin board. She was pretty sure it was Jill.

"Have a seat," he said, putting two glasses down on the table. "Sorry if I was a little short with ya just now. Can't be too careful—I don't want any bozos hangin' around here making mischief with my birds. So what brings you back here, Miss Clementine?"

She sipped her lemonade. It was good—more sour than sweet. "I need to know more about the ospreys."

Bo leaned back in his chair. "Amazing birds, aren't they?"

"But they're dying, right?"

He put down his glass. "First, like I told your school group, it was the DDT. Poison that was supposed to kill the mosquitoes. Well, it did, but the problem is that fish eat mosquitoes, so the DDT gets inside the fish. Each fish eats thousands of mosquitoes and then each bird eats hundreds, maybe thousands of fish. That means some birds get mighty big doses of DDT. Especially the ospreys, 'cause all they eat is fish."

"So the DDT poisoned the ospreys."

Bo tipped his chair even farther back and crossed his arms. "Well, sort of. The DDT made the female birds lay eggs with very thin shells. Then, when the mother birds tried to sit on the eggs, they broke."

"No chicks," Clem said.

"No chicks."

"Did the mother birds get upset?"

"Now that, I couldn't tell ya," said Bo. "I love those birds, but I have no idea what their thoughts are like."

"Are the eggs better now?"

"We think so," he answered. "Over the past couple years, we've seen some osprey chicks hatch in our nests. A few even fledged and went south. But we got another problem here on the Vineyard."

"What do you mean?" Clem set down her empty glass.

"Ospreys like to nest high up where they can get a good

view—360 degrees, if possible—and a clear landing. They love dead trees, like old pitch pines. But there's a lotta building goin' on, new vacation homes and whatnot, and those dead trees are the first thing to go when people clear the land."

Clem thought about all the new houses that had been built on Cobb's Lane. "What do the ospreys do then?"

"Find other places to build their nests. Sometimes the places they find are man-made, like chimneys and electrical power poles. When that happens, someone who doesn't know any better is probably gonna come and take the nest down—maybe even with some eggs in it."

"What can you do about that?"

"If I find out in time, I can go up and shoo the birds away. Get 'em to move to a safer place before they lay their eggs. But the ospreys need safer, better places to nest. So we put platforms on tall poles, in places where nobody will bother 'em.

Clem had seen these platforms before. She tried to remember where.

"Does it work? Do the birds use the platforms?"

"Sometimes. You have to be patient."

Clem thought about the bands in her pocket. Bo really did a lot for the ospreys. If anyone could tell her about her bird, it would be him. She pulled out the little baggie, untied it, and slid the bands onto the table.

"Do you know anything about these?"

Bo picked up the bands.

"Where'd ya find them?"

"I found a dead osprey on the beach in Menemsha. I cut them off."

"When was this?"

"A few weeks ago."

Bo turned the bands over in his hand, then placed them back on the table. He looked at her with a sharp expression. She wondered if she had been wrong to take the bands.

"What do you want to know?" he asked, finally.

"Where the bird came from. Who put the bands on it and why. How it died." She reached out and gingerly touched one of the bands. "I guess I thought whoever it was that banded it might like to know what happened to his osprey."

"When we band a bird, it doesn't mean we own it," said Bo.

"I know, but . . ."

He cut her off. "But you're right to think someone cares. Banding a bird kinda connects us to it, even though the bird is flying free."

"How do you think it died?"

Bo looked thoughtful. "Was it injured? Wounded? Could you tell if it had a broken wing or something?"

"Not that I could see."

Bo shook his head. "Hard to tell, then. Lotta things can happen."

"Do you know who put these bands on?"

"Yup. I do." Bo gave her a searching look.

"Who?"

"Daniel Willard. Goes to your school. He was here that day with your class."

Daniel! Clem remembered how Bo had called him by name when they visited Bird World. How Daniel had helped close Wendy's cage. How he'd known about the purple martins.

"Listen," said Bo. "He's a real good kid. This is gonna be a blow to him. But you need to tell him about what you found."

"I don't know . . ." Clem felt awkward. She wanted to talk to Daniel. But how could she tell him his bird was dead?

"You go talk to him." Bo looked serious.

"At school?"

He thought for a moment. "No, you probably should go to his house. Down on Menemsha Creek, by the Coast Guard Station. Can't miss it. Lives with his grandfather."

"Why?"

"That's the only folk he's got. Parents died a long time ago. Fishing accident." Bo pushed back his chair. "I've got to get to feedin' the birds."

Clem stood up and placed her glass in the sink. Bo walked her out to her bike.

"It's a good thing you came by," he said. "You go talk to Daniel. He'll want to know."

8

He Belongs to Himself

Clem had never been to the Coast Guard station, but she knew where it was. You had to turn left just after the Home Port Restaurant, the one where all the tourists went to eat lobster and watch the sunset. Adam liked to make fun of them, spending all this money for a sunset experience when anyone could walk down onto the beach and see it better for free.

The rising wind filled her nylon jacket like a spinnaker, slowing her down as she coasted around the bend. The wind carried the scent of rain and the sky was darkening. Perhaps a storm was coming.

She stopped her bike where the pavement ended, on the edge of a salt marsh. Beyond the marsh was the open water of Menemsha Pond. Wind rippled the tall grasses. This was the spot Bo had described, but she didn't see a house.

Then Clem spotted two parallel tire tracks running along

the edge of the marsh. She started down the tracks on foot and soon saw a ramshackle house. Grass had grown over the tires of an old rusty car parked in the turnaround. The paint on the house was peeling badly and two of the shutters dangled off their hinges. The sagging front porch faced the water.

It was just before dusk, so Clem couldn't tell if lights were on inside the house. But the smell of wood smoke told her someone was home.

Clem closed her eyes and took a breath to steady her nerves, then crossed the yard, stepped onto the creaky porch, and knocked.

Daniel opened the door. He was so tall, he ducked his head in the tiny doorway. He was wearing boots and a jacket, like he was heading out.

"Hi," he said.

"Hi."

She didn't know what to say next.

"Can we help you?" A deep voice creaked from inside the old house.

Daniel opened the door wider and took a step back.

Clem ducked inside. It was very warm. She smelled apples and old wood and pipe tobacco. After a moment, her eyes adjusted to the dim light. Shelves of books lined the cozy room. In the corner, a fire crackled inside a wood stove, and a very old man sat in a ragged armchair with a blanket over his legs.

Beneath his white hair, his thin face was crisscrossed with lines like a piece of paper that had been tightly crumpled, then opened and smoothed. He looked at Clem expectantly.

"My name is Clementine Harper. I'm in Daniel's grade at school."

The man nodded without saying anything.

"I was hoping to talk to Daniel." Clem stopped and looked at Daniel. She felt so awkward. She should have just waited until Monday and talked to him at school.

The old man spoke again. "What did you wish to speak with my grandson about?"

"Birds."

"Ah."

"Ospreys."

"I see." He appeared to consider this for a bit.

Daniel shifted uneasily from foot to foot.

"Why don't you take the young lady outside, Daniel? You are both dressed for the cold. Maybe she would like to see your bird tower."

Daniel didn't move.

His grandfather waved a hand. "Go on!"

At that, Daniel caught Clem's eye and gave just a hint of a smile. He opened the door for her and they stepped outside.

Clem felt a little easier outside. She took a deep breath. Gray as the afternoon was, it felt bright and refreshing after the house's dark, close interior. Gusts of wind bent the marsh grass low.

They stood side by side looking out, still locked in awkward silence. Daniel shoved his hands in his pockets. Clem realized he hadn't said a single word since "Hi."

"I'm sorry," she said. "I should have called first."

"No, don't be sorry," he said. "I'm pleased to see you."

Clem felt a little rush of happiness. Daniel was pleased to see her. Still, he didn't move, so she finally asked, "Were you going to show me your bird tower?"

"Of course." He shook his head and smiled—a bigger smile this time. This was the first time Clem had seen him really smile, and it was dazzling. Broad and white and just a little bit crooked. "Right this way!"

He leapt off the porch and crossed the sandy dirt lawn in a few long strides. Clem had to run to keep up. As they rounded the porch, she caught sight of a wooden shed on ten-foot stilts. Half of it was enclosed, and the other half looked more like a cage. There was a ladder attached to the side.

"That's a bird tower?"

"The technical name is 'hacking tower,'" Daniel answered, and scrambled up the ladder. He unlocked the padlock on the small door at the top and disappeared inside. Then he poked his head back out. "Would you like to come up?"

Clem climbed the ladder and peered into the unlit space. It

smelled strongly of ammonia, and she wrinkled up her nose.

Daniel grinned. "You'll get used to the smell. Come and meet Quinn."

Clem squeezed inside. The interior was bigger than she had expected. She could stand, although Daniel had to stoop. He was looking through a window covered with mesh. Clem went and stood by him. Now she could see into the cage side of the tower. There, standing on a bed of straw, was a bird.

An osprey, of course.

She was surprised again by the bird's size. It lifted its striped wings nervously and folded them back against its body. Opening its hooked beak, the bird made a loud, anxious, chirping sound, *"Kew-kew-kew-kew-kew!"* Its white chest feathers fluffed up, making the bird look even bigger.

The bird's eyes were not yellow, like those of Bo's osprey or the dead bird on the beach; they were bright orange. And they were staring at her. Clem moved a little closer to the mesh-covered window.

"Is it yours?" she asked.

"No."

"Whose is it, then?"

"He belongs to himself."

"I meant—where is he from?"

"I found Quinn on the ground near his nest in August. I think he fell when he was trying to fledge. To fly. I kept an eye on him for a while—his mother was still feeding him. But after a couple of days she gave up, I suppose. She went away and left him alone there. So I brought Quinn here."

Clem put her hand against the mesh.

Daniel touched her arm. "Don't," he said gently. "He is a wild bird."

"Will he bite?"

"No, I don't think so," said Daniel. "He can't reach you through the wire. You don't need to be afraid of him—but he needs to be afraid of you."

"I don't get it."

"If a young wild osprey starts to think of humans as family, he won't be able to return successfully to the wild."

"Family?"

Daniel leaned against the wall. "Quinn hasn't been with any other ospreys since he fell from the nest. They all went south. If a human were to feed him and pet him and act loving toward him, he might get confused and think he belonged among humans."

"Doesn't he need a family?"

Daniel thought about that for a moment.

"I don't know—although I imagine he would like one. But thinking of humans as family is dangerous for him. When he's older, he has to find a mate and create his own family."

"Don't you feed him?"

"Sometimes." Daniel opened an old cardboard box in the corner of the shed. "He can fly now, and most of the time he catches his own fish. At the beginning, I fed him, but I tried not to let him know it. I used this." He pulled a gray mitten out of the box and put it over his hand. It was painted to look like a bird's face, with the thumb and fingers colored black to resemble a beak.

"When I wear this, I guess you could say I'm his father. Or at least my hand is."

"What about his real father?"

"His father's name was Quitsa," said Daniel. "Short for Nashaquitsa—you know, the marsh where the boats are moored, just past Beetlebung Corner? It was one of my mother's favorite spots."

Clem nodded. She knew the place. It was one of her favorite spots, too.

"Quitsa was the first bird we raised here. He taught me everything I know about ospreys."

"What happened to him?"

Daniel paused, and Clem realized that she already knew the answer.

"He disappeared."

Daniel looked down at the floor. Clem had an urge to put her hand on his shoulder or his cheek or do something that would be comforting, but of course she didn't. Instead, she reached into her pocket and pulled out the bands. She held them out to him.

"Was he wearing these?"

Daniel's eyes widened. He took the bands out of their little bag and squinted at the numbers on the metal one. After a moment, he closed his fist around the bands and squeezed his eyes shut. Then he handed them back to her, and the expression in his blue eyes was sad and lost.

"Where did you get them?"

"I cut them off him. It was in September. I was walking on the beach, about a half mile east of Menemsha. He was—"

"Don't say it." Daniel cut her off. "I know."

9

Cicada in a Jar

Daniel turned away and faced the wall. His breathing sounded shaky. Clem looked away respectfully and tried to pretend she wasn't there. She felt awful. In his cage, Quinn shuffled and shrugged. Finally Daniel turned to look at her gravely. His blue eyes were now steady.

"Shall we go back outside? We'll be able to breathe better," he said.

"Yes, let's." She exhaled in relief.

They clambered down the ladder and made their way to the porch, where there were two old rockers. They sat side by side, facing the water.

"How did you know to bring the bands to me?" he asked.

"Bo Jameson told me," Clem answered.

He nodded, and they rocked in silence for a while.

"I met Bo about three and a half years ago," Daniel said finally. "He knew Grandfather, and he came here one day to ask if he could build a hacking tower on Grandfather's property. He said his own land was too far from the water and too deep in the woods for the birds to nest there."

Daniel spoke like someone in an old-fashioned book, Clem thought. Among the other kids at school, it sounded odd. But here, on this old porch, it was perfect.

"Why is it called a hacking tower?"

"Hacking means raising birds away from their parents, away from their original nest," he said. "It's a very old art. It was developed hundreds of years ago in Europe by falconers. They used hawks to hunt small game, like rabbits. By hacking, they could raise birds that were wild enough to hunt successfully and tame enough to return to their owners with their catch."

"So the birds treat the trainers like parents?"

"A little. At least, the new nest—the hacking tower— becomes home."

"Do you and Bo use the ospreys for hunting?"

Daniel laughed. "No. Although that would be interesting! Bo rescues ospreys that have lost their parents. He hopes they'll make a home on the Island, and maybe bring other birds here as well."

They rocked for a while, and the silence felt a little less awkward.

Clem asked Daniel some more questions and he told her some of what he knew about the ospreys. How they made their nests and had their babies in northern areas like New England and Canada, then migrated thousands of miles south to Mexico and South America for the winter. They returned north each spring, often to the very same nest. So if you could get one new pair of ospreys to make the Vineyard their home, their children would do the same, and their children's children, starting new families every spring.

Clem was fascinated—both by the birds and by Daniel. "How did Quitsa end up with you and Bo?"

Daniel suddenly looked serious. "He was one of three chicks born in a nest that his parents had built on an electric power pole. When a work crew took down the nest, they found the chicks, and one of them called Bo. Two chicks had already died by the time Bo got there. Quitsa was the only survivor. Bo brought him here."

Daniel described how he cared for the chick, feeding Quitsa raw fish that he chopped into tiny pieces at first, then larger and larger chunks as the bird got bigger. Quitsa grew fast, and by the time he was eight weeks old, he began to fly.

Clem had never had a pet, or any other animal to care for. "I wish I'd been there for that."

"It was fantastic to watch." He smiled. "For a few days he just jumped up and down over his nest, flapping his wings.

Developing his muscles. Then he started hovering, just a little.

"Finally one day Bo said Quitsa was ready. We opened the outside door of his cage and he stepped out onto that ledge and just jumped." Daniel's face lit up.

"He could fly? Just like that?"

Daniel laughed. "Actually, the first time out, he had to make a crash landing in the water. He wasn't strong enough. We had to wade out and grab him and bring him back. A couple of days later, we opened the gate again and that time he was ready. He took off into the sky."

"That must have been amazing."

Daniel was looking dreamily at the horizon, as if he could see the bird disappearing in the distance.

"But sad too? To see him go?" she asked.

"Well, he still had to learn to fish. When he came back to the nest, we gave him food, just as his parents would have done, until he had the skills to feed himself."

Clem asked about the bands.

"The colored plastic band allows us to make a tentative identification from a distance," said Daniel. "But technically, you can only make a firm identification by seeing the number on the metal band. It usually only happens after a bird dies . . ." His voice trailed off.

"I'm sorry—" Clem started to say.

"No, I'm glad you found him and saved the bands. Otherwise I might never have known where he ended up."

They rocked quietly for a few moments.

"So Quitsa came back after he went south?" Clem said.

"I tried not to get my hopes up. A lot of birds die during the migration. Hurricanes, hunters, you name it. But he made it back. And he brought a mate."

Clem laughed. "He got a wife down in Mexico."

Daniel smiled. "We called the female Noepe. It's the Indian name for Martha's Vineyard," he told her. He pronounced it *No–eh–pay*.

"They built a nest on one of Bo's platforms and had four chicks, but only one survived. A few weeks ago, I visited the nest and that's when I found Quinn." Daniel leaned forward in his chair to pick up a small pebble off the edge of the porch, then flung it into the pond.

"Noepe disappeared a couple of days later. I knew that Quinn would not survive unless I fed him, so I brought him back here."

Clem thought about the young bird, all alone on the ground. "Why did Noepe leave him?"

"He couldn't fly, and she probably couldn't risk waiting any longer to leave the Island and head south. She may return in the spring. Her nest is still there, waiting for her to come back and start another family."

"But her mate was Quitsa," said Clem. "Will she be able to find another?"

"Ospreys usually mate for life," he replied. "But if they lose their partner, they sometimes find another." He looked at Clem. "I hope that's what Noepe will do."

"I hope so, too." Clem was surprised at how much she meant it. She wanted to see Noepe, and watch her start a new family. "What about Quinn?"

"I want him to migrate. It's getting late in the year, but he still has time to head south. I think he's almost ready to leave."

"Won't it be hard to let him go?"

"Yes," he said. "It will."

"I remember once I had this cicada in a jar," said Clem, then stopped. It was silly to share this old story.

But Daniel stopped rocking and looked at her with interest.

Clem took a deep breath. "I was eight years old. I found a molting cicada on a tree behind our apartment house in Cambridge. It was attached to the bark, and I could see the new green cicada through a crack in the back of its old hard brown skin."

The cicada's progress was slow. Clem went inside and got a stool to sit on while she watched. She stayed there all afternoon, watching. Just before dusk, after the cicada got free of its old too-small skin and unfurled its wings, she placed a jar over the insect and brought it inside. Adam came into the kitchen and found her trying to punch holes in the lid with a can opener.

"I'm not sure you can keep him happy in there, sweet-heart," Adam said.

"Yes, I can." She placed a bottle cap filled with water and a handful of grass and leaves in the jar. But when Clem looked at the cicada the next morning, it hadn't moved a millimeter. Worried, she put the jar outside and unscrewed the lid. Still, the insect didn't move.

All day at school, Clem worried. She felt guilty. Had she killed the cicada? Maybe she gave it the wrong kind of leaves. Or too much water. Or maybe she shouldn't have put it in the jar at all.

But when Clem finally got home from school and ran to check the jar, she found it empty.

"I was so relieved! I know it was just a bug. But I would have felt so bad if I was responsible for its death. But I re-member I was sad that I didn't see it fly away."

"It will likely be the same with Quinn," said Daniel.

"You won't be there to see him go?"

"No," he answered. "Just like Quitsa, he'll fly farther and farther from the tower and then one day, when he feels ready, he won't come back."

Suddenly, Clem desperately wanted see Quinn fly. She had just remembered watching her first osprey dive for fish on

Menemsha Beach. She wanted to see that—and feel that awe—again.

"Can you let him out now?"

"Right now?"

"Please? I would love to see him fly."

Daniel thought about it. "He's been fishing already once today. But maybe he'd like to ride this breeze."

They walked back over to the hacking tower.

Daniel went to the cage side of the tower, stepped up onto a crossbar, reached overhead, and unhooked something. Then he came around and climbed the ladder. He unwound a rope that was secured to a cleat on the outside of the tower by the door. The rope led up over the roof. When it was free of the cleat, Daniel pulled on the rope. A door swung open on the front of the cage.

Quinn immediately came to the door. He looked around, fluffed out his feathers, and leapt.

Clem felt a rush of air as Quinn swooped from the tower, tucking back his legs. He spread those enormous wings—far broader than she had imagined when she saw him in the cage—and flapped them with a slow, powerful beat. He dropped to skim over the water, then rose, his tail feathers stretched straight behind him. His wings flapped smoothly, with a jaunty grace. The osprey veered left and flew over the peninsula.

"He's trying to locate an updraft," Daniel said, climbing down quickly.

Quinn stopped flapping and soared, gliding without a hint of effort.

"There, look, he found one." Daniel said.

He walked over and stood beside Clem. As they watched the osprey together, she almost felt like she was gliding too. And in her mind, she saw that jewel-green cicada, buzzing away on fresh new wings.

10

Something to Look Forward To

Clem was surprised to find the kitchen still dark when she got up at 7:15 a.m. It was Tuesday, Nora's day to go to Boston. Her mother was usually packed and ready to go by now. They always ate breakfast together and then Nora drove Clem to school and continued on into town to catch the boat.

Clem peeked into Nora's room. Her mother was still in bed, rolled like a mummy in the blanket, her long hair tangled on the pillow. "Nora?"

She didn't move. Clem walked to her side and shook her gently. "Nora?"

Nora's eyes fluttered open. Clem saw the confusion on her face. For a second, she wanted to climb into the bed and put her arms around her mother.

Then Nora snapped to attention. "What time is it?"

"Seven fifteen."

Eyes wild, Nora looked around the room, then threw the covers back and sprang out of the bed. "Why didn't you wake me sooner?

"I just woke up," said Clem. "Did you forget to wind your alarm clock?"

"No! It must be broken." Nora yanked open her drawers and grabbed clothes.

Clem backed out of the room. She got dressed quickly and made the lunches while Nora showered. She poured cornflakes into two bowls, added milk to her own bowl and began eating.

Nora rushed into the kitchen. "No time for breakfast."

"Don't you always tell me my body needs fuel to perform well?" Clem checked the clock. "We usually leave at 7:45. It's only 7:39. You can eat."

Nora hesitated. "Fine." She sank into the chair with her purse still on her shoulder. She poured the milk and took a couple of bites. "I'm ready. Time to go."

Clem jumped up. "Don't forget your lunch," she said, pointing to the brown bag on the counter.

Clem sat alone at lunch, as she often did. In good weather, the ninth graders usually ate in a grassy area beside the school. Sometimes Sandy joined her, but Sandy liked to circulate. Now that she knew Daniel, Clem thought she might sit with him sometimes, but that hadn't happened yet. She didn't see him on the grass. She had no idea where he ate his lunch.

"Hi."

She looked up from her book to see Jill standing right in front of her.

"May I?" her teacher asked, pointing to a spot on the ground next to Clem.

Surprised, Clem nodded.

Jill dropped her patchwork shoulder bag on the grass and sat down cross-legged. She pointed to *Under the Sea-Wind*, which lay open in Clem's lap. "What do you think?"

"I like the part about Rynchops best." The book was divided into three sections: one about a seabird, Rynchops, one about a mackerel, and one about an eel.

"I'm going to have to look at that book again," said Jill. "I read somewhere that it was Carson's favorite out of all the books she wrote." She rummaged through her bag and pulled out a lunch sack. "I heard you went back to Bo Jameson's."

"You did?" Clem thought about Sandy's comment about Jill and Bo being a couple. She was probably right.

"He told me you brought him some osprey bands." Jill unwrapped a sandwich. "So sad to find one of those beautiful birds dead. Bo said the bird was young. But he was glad you found it."

"Daniel was, too," said Clem.

Jill raised her eyebrows. "Oh, so you two have connected."

"He showed me the hacking tower."

Jill nodded. "Well, maybe you and Daniel can help me talk to the other students when we visit a nesting site." She took a bite of her sandwich, then dug into her big bag again. "If you are really interested in the ospreys and why they need our help, I have another book you might like."

She laid a book in front of Clem. The dust jacket was worn, like it had been read many times. The cover was green, with a simple drawing of some marsh grass and the title *Silent Spring*. Clem remembered the title. This was the book Jill had told them about at Bird World.

"It's by Rachel Carson, too," said Jill. "This was her last book, and her most important one. This is the book that got DDT banned in the U.S."

"Bo told me about DDT and the ospreys."

"Rachel Carson is one of my heroes. After she published this, the pesticide companies tried to ruin her. But she stood up to them." Jill tapped the cover. "*Silent Spring* is a challenging book. I don't usually recommend it to freshmen. You might not like it."

Clem picked up the book. Above the title was written "The author of THE SEA AROUND US and THE EDGE OF THE SEA questions our attempt to control the natural world about us."

"I think I'll like it," she said.

"Well, you can borrow it then." Jill closed her bag. "I've got to go. But do you mind if I ask you a question?"

"No."

"I hear your mother's a professor at Boston University."

"Yes. She teaches anthropology."

"How does she manage that, living out here?"

Clem explained about Nora's schedule, and how she commuted and stayed over in Boston one night a week.

"But your father lives in Ohio, right? So where do you go when your mother is off-island?"

"Nowhere," answered Clem.

"I mean, I know you stay on the Island, because you haven't missed any school. But who do you stay with?"

Clem wondered if Nora could get in trouble for leaving her alone. She didn't want that to happen. But she felt like she could trust Jill.

"I stay at home," she said.

"Alone?"

"Well, she checks in on me by phone. My father does, too."

"Oh," said Jill. "I see . . . and you feel safe?"

Clem paused, thinking about the dark woods outside the cottage at night. Then she nodded.

"Yes," she said firmly.

"Well, that's good then," said Jill. "See you inside."

Maybe, Clem thought, she should think of a better way to answer that question the next time someone asked.

As the students filed out at the end of science class, Jill handed Clem a folded slip of paper.

"In case you ever need anything," she said.

Clem opened the note and saw Jill had written her phone number on it. That was kind of weird—but nice, too. "Thanks." She zipped the paper into the pocket of her backpack and headed outside.

Daniel was near the back of the bus, looking out the window. Another boy sat next to him. Sandy was already sitting with someone, chattering cheerfully. Feeling awkward and disappointed, Clem took a seat alone near the front.

Most of the kids had already gotten off and Clem was counting the landmarks to her own stop, when someone dropped into the seat beside her. It was Daniel. He'd walked all the way up from the back of the bus to join her. He sat a little at an angle because his long legs didn't fit in the seat.

"Hi," she said, sure she was blushing.

"Hi." Daniel reached down to put his book bag on the floor. "I talked to Bo by phone last night. He said I should ask you to come with me when I visit him and the birds tomorrow after school."

"He told you to ask me?"

"Well . . ." Now it was Daniel's turn to blush a little. "It might have been my partly my idea."

"Oh."

"I mean, if you're not busy."

"Let me see . . ." Clem pulled her assignment book out of her backpack and paged through it like she was checking for conflicts.

"You probably have something else going on. We could go another time."

Clem looked up at him. "What time tomorrow?"

"Then you'll come?"

She smiled. "Of course!"

"Just get your bike right after school and I'll meet you at the end of Cobb's Lane."

Clem noticed that the bus wasn't moving. She looked up and saw the bus driver watching them the rearview mirror with an amused expression. This was her stop. Clem jumped up, flustered.

"Bye. See you tomorrow!" She took the steps two at a time, then turned and watched the bus disappear along North Road.

Finally, something to look forward to.

That night, after the check-in call with Nora, the phone rang again. It was Coco.

"So, I was thinking," she said. "You don't really like school there, right?"

"Well, kinda." Clem had told Coco about Beth.

"So why don't you tell Nora you want to come back to Cambridge? You could stay with me!"

"Your parents would let me live with you for the whole school year?"

"You know they love you, Clem!"

Clem heard a thump. Coco must have thrown herself back against the puffy pillows on her bed.

"Plus," Coco said, "you're so quiet, they probably wouldn't even notice you were here."

"Very funny." Clem considered the idea. Live with Coco! What could be better? They would have so much fun— it would be just like it used to be. They could be together every day. She could go to school with kids she knew. Plus, no fights with Nora. No Beth. No worries about nights alone on the Island.

But no Daniel. Clem could hardly believe she was thinking this—she barely knew him. But suddenly leaving the Island didn't seem so appealing.

"Coco, it sounds awesome," she said. "But I'm sure Nora wouldn't go for it."

"She'd say I'm going to corrupt you, wouldn't she?"

"Well, not exactly, but—"

"She'd be right! I'd corrupt you in the best possible way."

"I'm sure you would."

They both laughed.

"Well, think it over."

"Okay."

There was a long silence.

"Waaait," said Coco. "You're not telling me something. What's changed? Did that Beth girl switch schools? Get run over by a sailboat?"

"Nooo, but something did happen."

"Tell me, tell me!" begged Coco.

"Well, you know how I found that dead bird on the beach? And I cut off the bands and kept them?"

"Ugh, I remember."

"So I actually met the person who raised that bird and put the bands on its legs. You won't believe it. He's a boy at my school!"

"You're kidding! Is he cute?"

Coco probably wouldn't think so, Clem knew.

"Not really . . . I mean, not in the conventional way . . . but, I mean, maybe! He's tall. I guess he might be a little bit cute."

"Get a grip, Clem! You meet a boy and you can't tell me if he's cute or not?"

"He is, sort of. But kind of shy."

"Well, next time I talk to you I expect a full report: eye color, clothes, shoe size, everything. What's his name?"

"Daniel. And his eyes are blue."

"Ooh, I love blue eyes. He likes birds, huh?"

"Yeah. He raised the one that I found on the beach. He has a new one now. It's almost ready to migrate."

"Sounds like he's already talked to you a lot."

"I guess."

"Geez, did anybody ever tell you how frustrating you are to talk to? It's like pulling teeth!"

"Coco, if something happens, you'll be the first person I tell."

"Promise?"

"Promise."

11

Quitsa's Bands

The next afternoon, Clem didn't mind the long bike trip to Bird World. Daniel rode in front of her and kept looking back over his shoulder. Like he was making sure she was still there. Clem found this funny, and a little sweet.

They found Bo outside, feeding the birds.

"Well, look who's here," he said. "Give me a hand. Then we can get inside—it's gettin' chilly!"

Daniel knew what to do. He filled buckets with water and grain, giving one to Clem and carrying two by himself. As he swung the big heavy buckets, Clem saw how strong he was.

He knew all the birds by name, too.

"Hey there, Norma. Shad! Bluefish! Wendy! Step back! Don't be so greedy!"

As Daniel walked among the birds they squawked, fluffed out their feathers, and beat their wings. Clem hung back, a little nervous about their beaks and claws. But Daniel wasn't worried. A crow hopped up on his shoulder and he didn't flinch.

After the birds were fed, they followed Bo into the kitchen and sat at the green table. There was a full pot of coffee in the coffeemaker.

"Would you like some?" he asked, placing a mug in front of Clem.

"No, thanks." She watched as he poured Daniel a cup. "I'm not much of a coffee drinker."

"Try it like this." Bo poured a little coffee into her mug, then filled it to the top with warm milk from a pan on the stove. "You're gonna love it." He dumped in three spoons of sugar and sprinkled some cinnamon on the top.

Clem sipped it slowly, hugging the cup with her hands and letting the spicy steam warm her face. Bo was right—it tasted amazing.

"Bo," said Daniel, staring down into his mug. "Clementine brought me Quitsa's bands. She found him on the beach."

"I know." Bo's face was grave. "I'm sorry, son. I thought something like this might have happened. Quitsa wouldn't have left his wife and chickies alone if he could help it."

Daniel looked up. "What do you think killed him, Bo?"

"We saw him not too long before he died, right? You didn't notice anything wrong?"

Daniel shook his head.

"So he probably wasn't sick. And Miss Clem said he was, you know, intact. There've been cases where owls picked 'em right out of the air. But since he wasn't eaten, my guess is he drowned."

"Drowned?" Daniel looked surprised.

"Yeah. It happens." Bo leaned his chair back. "Sometimes an osprey catches a fish that's too heavy to fly with. It gets caught in the spicules." He looked at Clem. "That's the little hooks on their toes. They get into the fish's flesh and the osprey can't let go. Fish pulls 'em right under and the bird drowns."

"But he wasn't holding a fish when I found him," she said.

"Fish probably wriggled away after he drowned," Bo said.

Daniel nodded. "Then that's what happened. Quitsa died trying to get fish for Quinn." His mouth was set straight across, his lips pressed into a firm line. "I'm certain of it."

She suddenly remembered something. Daniel's parents had died while fishing. That's what Bo had said. Fishing to feed their family.

"You think Miss Clem here would like to see a nesting platform?" Bo pushed away his empty cup and stood up. "I was gonna check the one down at Lobsterville today, just to make sure it's shipshape."

"What do you think, Clementine?" Daniel looked at her.

"That sounds great."

Bo helped them hoist their bikes into the back of the pickup and they piled into the front seat. Clem sat between Bo and Daniel.

"You two are going to have to share the belt," said Bo. "I'm a good driver, but no sense taking any risks."

Daniel and Clem each grabbed a side of the lap belt. It was an old truck, and it didn't have the kind of retractable belts they put in the newer cars, just an adjustable buckle. Clem was glad she didn't have to look at Daniel as they connected the two sides of the buckle. Daniel tightened the strap and for a moment, his bare arm pressed against hers. The spot where they touched tingled, even after he moved his arm.

How could she describe Daniel to Coco? He was so different from other boys. Young and old at the same time. Awkward but strong. Blue eyes and blond hair and sunburned cheeks. How could she tell Coco all those things and make her understand?

For half the ride to Lobsterville, they sat squeezed shoulder to shoulder, pulled uncomfortably tight by the lap belt. Finally Daniel reached his left arm along the back of the seat behind Clem. Her shoulder fit perfectly into the space left beneath his outstretched arm and Clem felt like she could breathe again. As the truck rattled along, the sleeve of his worn T-shirt brushed softly against the back of her neck. Clem wanted to lean back and rest her head on his arm. Instead, she held it stiffly forward, away from the seat back.

Lighthouse Road traced the north shore of the Island from Gay Head to Lobsterville. Then it veered inland a short way before arriving in a dead end at Menemsha Pond. Clem loved this quiet spot, safe from the wind and surf. She and Nora and Adam had spent many lazy summer days there, playing in the shallow water, gathering shells, and reading on towels laid out on the sand.

They got out of the truck and stood at the edge of the parking area. The sun hung low in the blue sky. There were no people on the beach, just a line of dinghies and small sailboats dragged up into the tall grass and secured with ropes and chains to wait out the winter.

"Near here is one of the places where my people used to grow and harvest cranberries," said Bo. "Now the bogs are gone. But at least it's not wall-to-wall vacation houses, like down-island. Some of this land is protected."

Clem followed the direction of Bo's gaze out to the left, where beach grass, wild rosebushes, and low shrubs covered the land. She saw a tall wooden pole that looked like a telephone pole, topped by a platform. A giant nest built of twigs and branches sat on top of the platform. They walked over to the pole and Clem looked up. The platform was about twenty feet above her and the nest looked big enough for a pterodactyl.

"Let's give it a test." Bo wrapped his hands around the pole and tried to shake it.

Daniel went around to the other side and gave it a shake as well. The pole didn't budge.

"Good and solid. That's what I like to see." Bo looked up and frowned at the huge nest. "Daniel—run and get the ladder with Miss Clem."

They galloped back to the truck. Daniel stepped onto the running board and Clem clambered up on the bed. Together, they untied Bo's extension ladder and lowered it down.

They carried the light aluminum ladder along the beach, walking in step toward the sun, which hovered low over the horizon and filled their eyes. They climbed the dune and waded through the saw grass to the base of the pole. Bo helped them extend the ladder. Then he raised it and leaned it against the platform.

"I'll go up first, if you don't mind," he said, starting up the ladder. "You spot me, Daniel."

"Do you always check the nests like this?" asked Clem.

Daniel gripped the ladder, his eyes trained on Bo. "We usually take a look in the fall or winter, just to make sure everything's still good. Then in early summer we check for eggs. After they hatch, we go up again to put bands on the chicks."

The ladder shook a little and Daniel firmed his grip.

"The birds let you handle them?" she asked.

"They're usually not too happy about it. But they get over it quickly. Two summers ago, Bo moved a pair to this pole from another site. They were nesting on a piling in Menemsha Harbor, and all the fishing boats and the power yachts made it hard for them. The movie crew for *Jaws* was here, so the harbor was extra busy."

"I remember that," said Clem.

"Lookin' good up here!" Bo yelled, and started to back down the ladder.

"The parents kept getting frightened off by all the activity. Bo was afraid the chicks would starve. So he moved them over here in a boat—and the parents followed him the whole way."

Clem tried to imagine the scene. "Did you go with him?"

"No. I just watched from shore. I—I'm not fond of boats."

"I'm sorry," Clem said softly. She wished she knew more about what had happened to his parents.

"That's all right."

"Your turn, Clem." Bo reached the bottom of the ladder. "Daniel and I'll keep it steady for ya."

"Really?"

"Sure! You didn't come all this way for nothing, didja?"

"The nest is empty, right?" she asked.

"Well, there's no ospreys there. I'm not sure I'd call it empty, though," said Bo, winking at Daniel. "It's surprising what you find in these nests."

Clem stepped gingerly onto the ladder. The rungs felt solid and she began to climb. The spit of land between here and the beach was flat and open, without houses or trees. By the sixth step, she could see all the way to the Vineyard Sound. A few more rungs, and the masts of the fishing boats in Menemsha Harbor came into view. She felt dizzy—and nervous—and thrilled, all at once. Also a bit queasy. The ladder shifted a little and Clem froze.

"Don't worry, we got ya!" Bo yelled.

A few more rungs and she reached the top of the ladder. Now Clem had the same sweeping view as the birds. All the way to wide-open water and beyond. All the way to the hazy green Elizabeth Islands.

The giant, messy nest reached beyond the edge of the platform. Some of the branches were so big that she couldn't imagine how the birds carried them here. Clem leaned back slightly to peer over the rim of the nest.

Dried bird droppings covered the branches. She caught a sharp whiff of the same ammonia smell she remembered from Quinn's tower. Then she noticed bits of color among the branches.

"What's in here? Something orange . . . and some blue!" She hoisted herself a little higher.

"Careful!" Bo yelled. "Grab the platform, not the nest! Those birds don't use screwdrivers!"

Clem grasped the platform and studied the nest. She spotted dried seaweed, leaves, and a lot of other flotsam. Tiny bones—fish bones, probably. A piece of nylon rope. Some torn blue plastic—a piece of a tarpaulin? A child's plastic sand shovel. And, on the far side of the nest, something pink—the leg of a doll.

"What the heck?" she yelled. "Where'd this stuff come from?"

"Let's talk down here!" said Bo.

Clem backed down. Once on the ground, she looked at Bo. "Did you and Daniel put those things in there?"

"Nah." Bo grinned. "The birds did that. That's the osprey for ya. Real good foragers. Some might even call 'em dirty little thieves."

He chuckled and grabbed the ladder, lowering it to the ground. Daniel and Clem picked it up. They walked to the truck with the sun at their backs, their tall shadows laying out a path before them.

It was nearly six o'clock, so Bo drove them home. He told them that State Road, with all its twists and turns, was no place for a bicycle in the dusk.

Clem shared the seatbelt with Daniel again. This time, he put his arm along the top of the seat right from the start. While she listened to Bo talk—and he talked enough for the three of them—Daniel's arm came to rest lightly on her shoulder.

"That nesting pole was one of my first, and it's still one of the best," said Bo. "The birds like havin' the pond and the ocean for fishing. We've had three families fledge from that site."

Clem leaned back, just a little, to rest her head against Daniel's arm.

Bo kept talking. "I'd like to get two or three more poles up this winter, so we'll be ready for more birds. Daniel and I could sure use some help with that."

Clem felt a little thrill. "You mean me?"

"You see anybody else in this truck?"

Clem turned her head and looked at Daniel. He raised his eyebrows as if to say, "Why not?"

She turned back to Bo. "Okay, I guess!"

"Well then, it's settled. Welcome aboard." Bo took his right hand off the steering wheel and extended it to Clem.

She took his hand. He gave her a firm shake.

"One of these days, you're gonna see osprey nests all along

the shores of the Vineyard." Bo nodded his head. "That will be a grand sight."

When Bo pulled up in front of Clem's cottage, Daniel hopped out and opened the tailgate. They rolled Clem's bike to the edge, then lifted it down together. Just before Daniel got back into the cab, Clem grabbed his arm. She pulled the bands out of her pocket and pressed them into his palm.

"Here. You should have these."

"Oh," he said, looking down at the bands and then into her face with a serious expression. "Thank you."

12

Happy Thanksgiving

Clem had been looking forward to Thanksgiving for just one reason: Adam. She begged to go with Nora to pick him up at the Boston airport the day before Thanksgiving. But her mother wouldn't let her miss school.

After school on Wednesday, Clem decided to meet them at the ferry. She wanted to be there the second Adam set foot on the Island. She ignored the bus and walked out to the road that led into town and stuck out her thumb.

You hardly ever saw hitchhikers on the mainland—it wasn't safe to get in a stranger's car. But on the Vineyard, people did it all the time. It was like the rules were different here. People felt safer on the Vineyard. They left keys dangling from the ignition in their cars and didn't lock their houses. Clem had hitched on the Island with Adam, lots of times, but she'd never done it on her own. She felt daring. And a little uneasy.

Within five minutes, a rusty sedan slowed and pulled to a stop. The driver was a grandmotherly woman with fluffy gray hair and a poodle beside her on the seat. Clem let out a little sigh of relief.

"I hope you don't mind riding with Jingles!" the lady trilled.

On the way into town, the chatty lady tried to start a conversation several times, but Clem felt too excited to gab. She patted the dog and looked out the window. She couldn't wait to see Adam.

Clem ran onto the pier just as the ferry lumbered into the slip, bumping back and forth between the pilings like a pinball. Right away, she saw Adam and Nora. They stood together on the upper deck, leaning against the railing and looking toward town. Nora wore Adam's blue down jacket and he had his arm slung across her shoulders. Her long hair flew about in the wind and her cheeks were pink. Adam had grown a beard. Nora said a few words and he laughed. Clem felt the ping of something tight releasing inside her chest.

"Adam!" She waved and jumped.

He grinned at Clem and gave her a big two-armed wave.

In a moment, he came charging down the gangplank, wearing a giant backpack and pulling Nora by the hand. Clem ran to him and he smothered her in a giant hug.

"Clem-baby!"

Clem slapped his cheek happily. "I'm not your baby!"

"Sunshine, then!" Adam smiled. The beard made his teeth look even whiter than she remembered.

They moved to where the old Dart was parked, walking together, with Clem in the middle. In the car, it felt good to sit in her usual spot, right between Adam and Nora on the big front seat. Nobody made her wear a seatbelt. Adam put his right arm around Clem's shoulders while he drove. Every time he needed to shift gears, Clem ducked her head so he could reach over. She kept sneaking looks at his furry beard.

"You've grown, what, seven or eight inches since I saw you?" he joked. "It seems like just last year I could drive this car with you on my lap!"

"You never did that!" said Nora. "Did you?"

"Whoops, I forgot—that was supposed to be a secret!" Adam winked at Clem. "Seriously, when did you get so grown-up looking?"

Did she look different? Clem hadn't grown much taller over the summer. But her body was changing. She'd been wearing a bra for a while, but now she actually needed it. And the rest of her wasn't so stick-straight any more, either. Could Adam see that, even through all her heavy winter clothing? It was a little embarrassing to think he would notice.

But she was different inside, too. She felt more grown-up.

She liked sitting on the beach alone, with her thoughts. She could find her way around the Island by herself, and had spent all those nights alone when Nora went to Boston. And then there was Daniel.

Could Adam see all that?

He had changed, too, she thought. Clem liked the rugged look of his beard. She guessed that Nora liked it too. Instead of looking exhausted and worn-out, Nora seemed lit from inside. Clem nestled a little deeper between them.

"By the way, how did you get to the ferry?" Adam asked.

Clem had been hoping they wouldn't ask. "Oh, I caught a ride."

"As in, a friend gave you a ride?"

"Um, no. I hitchhiked."

"You what?" Adam's eyebrows shot up. He looked at Nora. "Are you letting her thumb around the Island now?"

Her mother shook her head.

"Nora didn't know," said Clem. "It was my decision. I don't see what's wrong with it. I've hitched with you plenty of times."

Adam took his arm off her shoulder and put his right hand back on the steering wheel. "That's different. I know the Vineyard seems safe, but this isn't the sixties anymore. This is the seventies. Things happen."

"Adam, let's talk about this later," said Nora, putting her hand on Clem's knee.

Clem felt betrayed. She had figured Adam would see her point of view. That he would be impressed by her self-sufficiency. Instead, he acted like he was in charge, even though he'd been gone for months. But she didn't want to start Adam's visit with an argument.

They were all silent for a few minutes.

Adam slowed. A gaggle of wild turkeys ambled across the road in front of them, ignoring the Dart.

Clem didn't like the quiet in the car.

"I guess they know they've got nothing to fear from us," she joked. They never ate turkey on Thanksgiving—they had their own family traditions. She waved at the birds. "Happy Thanksgiving, turkeys! Gobble in peace!"

Adam and Nora both chuckled. Everything felt fine again.

"Have you got our fishing rods all tuned up?" Adam asked.

"Yup. Mine was pretty tangled but I think it's good to go now."

Last summer, Adam had taught her to surf cast for stripers and bluefish. He bought Clem her own tackle and they studied the tide charts together. He showed her how to pull the rod back and then flick the line out over the water. She learned how to bait the hook with live eels, which she hated. So far, Clem hadn't caught anything. Part of her hoped it would stay that way. She loved to eat fish, but she didn't like the idea of killing one.

They always spent Thanksgiving on the Vineyard, and they always ate the same thing: lobster. Nora bought the lobsters the night before, since Larsen's and Poole's fish markets were closed on Thanksgiving Day. Then they kept them alive in a bucket of ocean water on the porch overnight.

Then, right before dinner, when Adam lugged the bucket into the kitchen, Clem always ran outside and waited under the big tree. She couldn't watch Adam lower the lobsters into the pot of boiling water. He said they didn't feel it, but she didn't believe him.

Just like every other Thanksgiving, they woke up early. Adam built a fire to warm up the cottage, then they made bread together.

Clem was in charge of the yeast, and she always tested the water temperature against the inside of her wrist the way Grammy Jo—Adam's mother—taught her. If the water was too hot, the yeast would die. If it was too cold, they wouldn't grow. She poured the warm water into a big ceramic bowl and added the little packet of yeast granules. She loved watching the yeast bubble and foam as it came to life.

Next, they mixed together the flour, water, salt, shortening, and yeast. Nora and Adam and Clem took turns kneading. After the second rising, Clem punched down the dough, pounding out the air until the puffy dough collapsed in on itself. Then she shaped the loaves for the final rising, pressing the rounds of dough flat and pulling up the sides and ends and pinching it all together, then turning them over to hide the seam. When the loaves were ready to bake, they put the big lobster pot on the stove. It took a long time for so much water to come to a boil.

While they waited for the water, they made salad, melted butter and skimmed off the foam, sliced lemons, and set the table. Everyone was busy, and the cottage filled with the rich, comforting aroma of baking bread.

Clem loved the holiday rituals. Performing the same tasks each year, smelling the same smells, tasting the same tastes—for a moment she could imagine that she was still eleven, or ten, or eight, or younger. So much had changed. But when she was kneading the Thanksgiving bread, everything seemed the same.

After the feast, they snuggled under a blanket and did a crossword puzzle together, with Adam reading out the clues and Nora and Clem racing to get the words. Just like they did every year.

Clem climbed into bed that night feeling peaceful. Soon, though, she heard Adam and Nora out on the porch, speaking in low voices. She couldn't hear what they were saying, but the sound of their tight whispers made her heart beat faster. She got up, opened her door, and closed it again, loudly enough for them to hear it and know that she was awake.

The voices stopped.

13

Here for the Holiday

At six a.m. Friday, Adam knocked on her bedroom door.

"Time to go fishing, Sunshine. I'll be in the kitchen," he whispered loudly.

Her room was dark and chilly. Clem pulled on jeans, a turtleneck, and a thick Irish sweater over her long johns. She stumbled into the kitchen, wincing at the fluorescent light. Adam poured her a cup of hot chocolate.

As much as she hated getting up early in the cold, Clem had been looking forward to fishing with Adam. They would stand next to each other on the beach, looking out at the water, waiting for the right moment to cast. Then they would watch their lines for the sudden stiffening that meant a fish had been hooked.

And they would talk. They could always talk better side by

side. Like rocking with Daniel on his porch. It was easier than face to face.

When they got to Squibnocket, they put on their hip waders over their jeans—it was far too late in the year to surf cast in shorts and bare feet, the way they did in the summer—and clambered over the rocks to the beach.

The sun was just coming up and the water glowed. The beach always seemed to get light before the rest of the world in the early morning.

They hoped to catch striped bass—beautiful silvery fish that fed on small fry near the surface of the water and fought hard when hooked. Clem looked for the signs of a good spot for surface feeders: waves that didn't break too close to shore and deposits of gravel and broken sand flea shells on the beach. She studied the waves through her binoculars. You didn't want to see too much sand in the waves, because the fish won't feed in places where the surf pulls up the bottom. She had learned all this from Adam.

Out of the corner of her eye, Clem noticed something moving about a hundred yards down the beach. She turned and raised the binoculars. She saw a person, sitting on a large rock and looking out to sea, also through binoculars. She rolled the focus knob and saw a mop of bright-blond hair.

Daniel.

What was Daniel doing on the beach? He must have come

by bicycle, although she hadn't noticed his bike in the parking lot. Then she wondered if he had seen her yet.

Clem felt a little guilty. Yesterday had been a good day for her—at least until nighttime. But it must have been lonely for Daniel and his grandfather. Just two people sharing a Thanksgiving dinner, without Daniel's mother and father. If they even had a special meal. She hadn't even thought about how hard the holiday must be for him.

"Clem?" Adam grabbed her hook, which was swinging loose from her pole.

She turned to look at him.

He frowned. "You got something on your mind?"

"No . . . yes. I was just thinking."

"About what?"

"Oh, I don't know. Nothing, really." Clem didn't feel like telling Adam about Daniel. She used to share everything with her father, but things were different now.

"You know our situation is temporary, don't you?" Adam's frown grew deeper. "That Nora and I are working on figuring out how to all be together again soon?"

"I know," Clem replied.

But she didn't. When they were cooking together on Thanksgiving, she thought that they could all be happy again, the way they were before. But hearing Nora and Adam argue last night had chased away that hope and left her feeling cold inside. She looked at Adam and felt as if she were viewing him through the wrong end of her binoculars. He was far away, and getting farther by the minute.

"Wait here for me, okay? I'll be right back."

"What?" Adam looked confused.

"I want to say hello to someone." Clem put down her rod and walked down the beach toward Daniel. She knew Adam was watching but he didn't follow and she didn't turn around.

When she got to the big rock, Daniel looked over without surprise, then back out to sea.

"Are you looking for Quinn?" she asked.

"I guess so. But I don't really expect to see him. He hasn't been back to the nest in a few days."

"Do you think he flew south?"

"I hope he did. He doesn't have much time to get away from here before the winter weather sets in."

"You'll miss him, won't you?"

"He'll be back."

Daniel gestured toward Adam with his chin. "Is that your father over there?"

"Yes. He's here for the holiday."

"Are you enjoying your time with him?"

"Come and meet him! I'd like to introduce you."

Daniel reddened. "I think . . . I think I'd rather not, if you don't mind too much."

"Oh. That's fine. Of course." She bent down to pick up a shiny jingle shell, letting her hair swing forward to hide her face. Maybe she shouldn't have asked. Again, she felt the urge to reach out to Daniel—put her hand on his shoulder, maybe. Instead, she handed him the little shell.

"I'd better get back."

"All right." Daniel examined the golden disc in his palm.

"Any advice for the fishermen?"

"Follow the birds. They know where the fish are." Daniel looked up at her with a tentative grin.

She pushed her hair out of her eyes and smiled back.

On Sunday morning, Clem sat on the edge of Nora and Adam's bed—she had begun to think of it as Nora's bed, but right now it was Adam's, too. He knelt on the floor, rolling his clothes and arranging them in his backpack.

"I wish you didn't have to go."

"I know," said Adam. "Me, too."

"Are you going to stay longer at Christmas?"

Adam pulled a shirt out of the pack, shook it, and rolled it up again before he answered.

"Clem, we haven't figured out yet what we're going to do about Christmas. I've been invited to speak at a conference in San Francisco the week before. So it's going to be awfully hard to get back here in time for Christmas Day. And with OSU being on the quarter system, our break is really short. Plus, the flights are incredibly expensive around the holidays. You know my friend Craig lives in Oakland. He asked me to visit him and his wife for Christmas."

It took Clem a moment to understand what Adam was saying. "Wait . . . so you might not be here for Christmas?" Her eyes pricked with tears. She blinked quickly to stop them from falling.

Christmas was her favorite holiday. The three of them always spent it together in just the same way. On Christmas Eve, they sat together and listened to the church service on the radio—the only religious thing they ever did—and the organ music would surround them like a velvet cloud. In the morning, they exchanged gifts. Last year, she'd made a needlepoint sampler for Nora and she'd knitted a scarf for Adam—almost six feet long and warm, with only a few bumpy spots. He'd worn it every day for the rest of the winter. They gave her books, and usually one special present. Last year, her gift had been her precious ten-speed bike. They baked muffins, took a long walk, visited Nana or Grammy Joe, and came back home to play board games far into the night.

"You have to come for Christmas!"

"Well, I don't really know yet. We're just going to have to see."

Adam sat back on his heels and looked up at Clem, almost reluctantly. Like he was afraid to meet her eyes. Like he didn't want to see how hurt she was.

Then he went back to his packing.

14

A Reluctant Activist

In December, the days grew colder and Clem saw a different Martha's Vineyard. The grassy meadows at Long Point turned golden brown. Bare tangles of purplish-brown blueberry bushes lined Cobb's Lane. The blue ocean turned greenish gray. Now that the trees had shed their leaves, Clem caught glimpses of the ocean in places where she had never known the water was so near.

In Vineyard Haven, where they bought their groceries, the dark windows of the boutiques and souvenir shops were either empty or swirled with soap. Only stores that sold essential items like food or medicine or hardware stayed open in the winter. The sidewalks were deserted.

The days got too short for Clem and Daniel to ride their bikes to Bo's after school and still get home by dark. On Tuesdays, when Nora was in Boston, Clem got off the bus at

Daniel's stop and Bo picked them up in his truck. They went to his house and helped clean the cages or distribute feed. Sometimes they checked the nesting poles. Bo made them wear bright orange caps, since it was deer hunting season.

Then Bo cooked them dinner. He always brought Clem home in time for her check-in call with Adam or Nora.

"You don't always have to feed me when Nora's gone, you know," Clem told him. "I can manage on my own."

"But why would you?" Bo responded. "What young lady in her right mind would turn down the chance to share a meal with a coupla fine male specimens like Daniel and myself?" He winked at Daniel.

On other days, when Nora was deep in her writing, Clem would go to Daniel's after school to do homework. They sat across from one another at the massive, scarred wooden table that Daniel and his grandfather used as a dining table, writing desk, and work surface. They drank instant coffee (Daniel) and hot chocolate (Clem). The table and the heavy dark wood chairs seemed to have been in the same spot for a hundred years. To Clem, they felt solid and safe.

Mr. Willard usually sat in his raggedy armchair in the corner by the wood stove, chewing on his unlit pipe, reading and commenting aloud from time to time.

He seemed to know everything, and when Clem was stuck, he could always help—whether it was a science question or a vocabulary word. She quickly learned, though, that if she asked a question, they would be discussing the topic for a while.

"Mr. Willard, why are cranberries such an important crop in Massachusetts?"

"That's a very interesting question, Clementine. The cranberry is one of only a handful of fruits that are native to New England. Another grows right here in our yard. Do you know what it is?"

"Blueberries," Clem said quickly. She and Nora and Adam had spent many August mornings picking blueberries on Tea Lane.

Then Mr. Willard told them about how the Indians used to sell their cranberry harvest in New Bedford each year to pay for food that would get them through the winter. He described Cranberry Day, the Wampanoag festival that marked the end of summer. After the festival, the tribe migrated away from the shore to the interior of the Island for the winter season.

Once Mr. Willard set aside his book and began telling stories, Daniel and Clem put down their pencils. Daniel's grandfather had lived on the Island his whole life, and Clem loved to hear his tales. She also loved his accent, with its broad vowels and sharp consonants.

Daniel's own story came out slowly, in bits and pieces. Some of the details Clem got from Mr. Willard, some from Sandy at school. Daniel didn't speak of his parents. But Clem learned that his father (Mr. Willard's son) and mother had owned a fishing boat. They made their living by selling the fish they caught. Mr. Willard looked after Daniel during their fishing runs. Sometimes they were gone as long as a week. When Daniel was two, his parents were caught in a terrible storm on the ocean. They radioed for help, but by the time the Coast Guard reached their boat, they were gone. Washed overboard and drowned, it was assumed.

A few weeks later, Mr. Willard became Daniel's guardian. There was nobody else to care for him—Daniel's mother hadn't spoken to her family for years. Mr. Willard simply went to the courthouse and signed some papers, adopting Daniel.

Daniel told Clem that he had been homeschooled by his grandfather until the eighth grade. Lots of reading, writing, and nature study. That explained why Daniel spoke so formally, Clem had decided. He had grown up with only books and his grandfather for companions.

Then, a little over a year ago, Mr. Willard suddenly decided to send Daniel to school. He told Daniel he was simply too old to be his only teacher, but Daniel thought his grandfather wanted him to make some friends.

That didn't come easily, though. He told Clem she was his first friend at school. Knowing this made her feel sad for him, but glad at the same time. As if Daniel belonged just to her. She didn't have to share him with anyone.

Still, they didn't hang out together at school. It wasn't something they had talked about, but Clem figured that they both felt the same way. If they started sitting together in class, kids would tease them about being a "couple." In fact, Beth had already called them "lovebirds." Twice.

They weren't a couple. Not in that way. Some days, when they brushed hands accidentally or leaned together over a homework problem, she felt a jolt of excitement. Other times, there was just a comfortable feeling of friendship—like having a brother.

It was too much to sort out at school, where everybody else could see. So she didn't sit with him at school or save a seat for him on the bus.

Sometimes, though, she would look over and see Daniel reading or staring out the window. She felt a little lonely then.

One afternoon at Daniel's house, Clem finished her homework early. Daniel was still working, so she pulled out *Silent Spring* and found her place, about halfway through the book. As she started reading, Mr. Willard eased himself out of his chair and crossed the room to stand behind her.

"Well, that's a fine choice," he said. "It just might be the most important book written in my lifetime. Did you know that Daniel read it, too, around the time he started working with the birds?"

Daniel looked up from his history textbook.

"Are you enjoying it?" Mr. Willard asked.

"Well, I don't know if enjoying is the right word," Clem answered. "The first chapter was scary." Called "A Fable for Tomorrow," the chapter described a future where all the animals were dying of chemical poisoning. "And after that it's kind of slow going. Not like her first book."

"Ah, *Under the Sea-Wind.* That was Miss Carson's personal favorite of all her books." Mr. Willard turned and clumped across the floor to the bookcase that ran along an entire wall of the room. "It's been almost forgotten in the hoopla over *Silent Spring*. But *Sea-Wind* is lovely, isn't it? Gives one a sense of why she became a reluctant activist."

"Reluctant?" asked Clem.

"Oh, yes. Miss Carson wasn't always planning to change the world. She started out with a simple love of the sea—just like you and Daniel." He pulled down a book and returned to his chair, riffling through the pages. "Will you indulge me?"

"Go ahead, Grandfather," said Daniel. "You know you are going to read it whether we want you to or not."

"I don't know why I tolerate such impudence." Mr. Willard cleared his throat.

Daniel smiled at Clem. She saw that crooked smile more often these days.

"Here it is. This is from an essay Miss Carson wrote for *Holiday* magazine in 1958. She called it 'Our Ever-Changing Shore.' Allow me to read a passage." He pressed the book flat in his lap with one hand.

Clem put *Silent Spring* down on the table. She liked hearing Mr. Willard read aloud.

In his deep, rumbling voice, he started reading about the spirit of the sea. Rachel Carson said that you couldn't see it when you sat on the beach on a nice, sunny day getting a tan. To really know the sea, you had to be there at other times. At sunrise or at midnight or during a storm, when there was nobody around for miles and miles.

" 'For the ocean has nothing to do with humanity,' " Mr. Willard finished, this finger coming to a stop at the bottom of the page. " 'It is supremely unaware of man.' "

Those *were* the best times to be on the beach, Clem thought. Wild and windy days, when the clouds turned dark and heavy and big waves crashed recklessly on giant rocks. Or the early mornings when the water glowed mysteriously and blended with the sky. In those moments she almost felt her own edges blurring . . . as if she, too, could flow like water or blow like wind.

Mr. Willard turned a page. "There's a whole section here

where the author describes the fascinating mating habits of the horseshoe crab, which has been laying its eggs on the beach at peak tide under the full moon since the Paleozoic era."

He looked up at them. "How long ago was that, Daniel?"

Daniel closed one eye in a squint, which meant he was thinking. "About 550 to 300 million years ago?"

"Close enough," said Mr. Willard. "Miss Carson wants us to remember that these creatures have been on this planet much longer than humans. And after people have vanished from the earth, the horseshoe crabs will probably still be crawling out of the ocean to lay their eggs." He got a faraway look in his eyes. "Whenever I see those sturdy creatures, I feel as though I am gazing backward in time. A million years ago, I could have been standing on a beach watching the same thing."

Mr. Willard looked at Clem with his busy eyebrows raised, almost as if he expected her to answer. Then he smiled, looked back down at the book, and continued reading silently.

Clem thought about what he had said. She knew that feeling! She had often sat on a rock at the beach, watching the waves lap, one after the other, each a little higher than the last, and wondered whether someone else had sat on the same rock or stood in exactly that spot a hundred years ago and watched the waves, too.

Mr. Willard looked up from his reading. "Well, I now see I was wrong," he said. "Miss Carson was an activist back then, as well. She argues on the very next page that some places along the seashore needs to be left forever wild, the way they would have been if people had not come and changed them. Here's how she expresses it: 'For there remains, in this space-age universe, the possibility that man's way is not always best.' " He closed the book.

Was there any place on earth that had not been changed by humans? Not the Vineyard, Clem thought. Even on her favorite, most difficult-to-get-to beaches, she found ugly man-made things. Old buoys and torn fishing nets. Broken glass bottles— brown and green and clear. Raggedy burst balloons still attached to bits of string or ribbon.

Clem knew that the children who let those balloons float away into the sky never thought about what happened after that. But what about the adults who tossed bottles and cans and garbage into the water?

She felt a wash of sadness. Things were perfect once. Why couldn't people just let them stay that way?

15

You Understand, Don't You?

When Clem got home that evening, Nora was working in her room with the door shut. There was a letter from Adam on the kitchen table. Clem sat down and tore it open.

Sunshine!

It's hard to believe Thanksgiving was just three weeks ago. It seems like an eternity since our lobster feast, and since I saw you standing at the ferry slip, looking old enough to be one of my students.

Well, almost old enough. You're growing so fast, you make your old man feel like an old man.

Adam went on to write about fall in Ohio, how everyone there was crazy about Ohio State football, and how he had been nominated for an award for his new poetry manuscript. He had tons of news.

Then, at the end of the letter, he wrote this:

Sunshine, I'm sorry but I won't be with you and Nora for Christmas this year. You know the conference I told you about in California? Well, thanks to my Cahill Prize nomination, I've been asked to present at the conference, and three Bay Area bookstores have invited me to give readings! It's very flattering—but also useful. I'll have a chance to meet journal editors, and critics, and faculty from other colleges . . . people who can help me in my career. One of the readings is on December 28, so it makes sense to stay in Frisco a few days longer and spend Christmas with my college friend Joe and his family.

I'll miss you and Nora very much, and I'll think of you both gathered around the tree at Nana's on Christmas Day. You understand, don't you, Sunshine? We'll find another time to see each other. Soon, okay?

xoxo

Adam

Clem crumpled the letter and dropped it on the table. She got up and took a few steps toward Nora's room, and then stopped.

If Nora didn't know about Adam, then Clem didn't want to tell her. That was Adam's job. And if Nora did know, and hadn't told her, then . . . Clem got angry just thinking about it. In any case, talking to Nora would make her feel worse.

Clem picked up the phone and carried it into her room,

stretching out the cord. She sat on the floor with her back against the wall and dialed. Coco picked up right away.

"Coco," Clem whispered, "I wish you would come and visit RIGHT NOW."

"I miss you too, Island Girl. What's going on?"

"Nothing. I'm just—things are—I . . ."

"You're still worried about Adam and Nora, aren't you?"

"I just got a letter from Adam." Clem's eyes teared up. She grabbed a Kleenex.

"And?"

"He's not even coming home for Christmas!"

"Oh, Clem." Coco knew how much she loved Christmas. "That's really awful. I'm sorry."

Clem swiped at her eyes and sniffed.

"Oh, don't cry! It's not that bad," Coco said. "Who needs Adam, anyway?" Her voice brightened. "Maybe you can come with me and my folks to the Bahamas! It's going to be psyche-delic!"

Clem pictured them together in their swimsuits on a white beach with palm trees.

"I wish."

"No, really! My parents would love it!"

Nora and Adam couldn't afford a trip like that, and Nora would never let Coco's parents pay. Plus, it was crazy. Christmas was just two weeks away.

"That sounds so great, Coco. But it's not gonna happen. Plus, even though I'm mad at Nora, I can't leave her alone at Christmas."

"Is she really sad?"

"I guess. I don't know. We don't talk about it."

"Clementine?" Nora called from her room. "Are you getting off the phone?"

Clem covered the mouthpiece with her hand and yelled, "In a minute!" Then she told Coco, "Nora's going to kick me off the phone."

"Wait! Before you go, tell me . . . What's going on with that Daniel guy? He make a move yet?"

"No, it's not like that. What about you? Do you still like that guy in your French class?"

"No, he's old news. But back to you. What about Daniel?"

"We've been hanging out, yeah."

"And?"

"He's really nice, Coco."

"It sounds like there's a 'but' coming."

"No! There's no 'but.' He's great."

"So are you falling for him?"

"Maybe . . . I don't know! Sometimes I think I am, and sometimes I think he feels the same way, but other times it's so awkward! We can't even look at each other at school. And I'm not sure whether I want it to be, you know, romantic. It's like . . . I feel good when I'm hanging out with him. And Bo. And his grandfather even."

"You are so weird."

"It's crazy, Coco. Sometimes I want to kiss him, and sometimes I feel like he's the brother I never had."

"Trust me, Clem, if you want to kiss him, you don't think of him like a brother." Coco laughed. "I'm pretty sure you're nuts about him. And I bet he's crazy about you, too. You're probably the best thing that ever happened to him!"

"I don't know about that."

"I do. Listen, if I don't talk to you before Christmas, try and have a good time, okay? Put a picture of Adam on the wall and poke pins in it or something."

"Coco!" Clem laughed. "I hope you have a really good time in the Bahamas."

And she really did hope that. But, even more, she wished Coco was here. When she talked, Coco really listened. And nobody knew her like Coco—not Daniel, or Sandy, or Nora. Not even Adam.

Maybe Adam least of all.

16

Sugar Helps

The bell on the door of Caldwell's Bakery jingled merrily as Bo pulled it open for Clem and Daniel. Outside, it was still dark and bitter cold, but the bakery was bright and warm. Clem's stomach growled as she inhaled the sweet, cinnamony smell of something baking in the oven. Glazed doughnuts and apple turnovers and crisp crullers filled the glass display case. Artie Caldwell lumbered out of the kitchen. He wiped his hands on the white apron that covered his broad belly like a tablecloth.

"Bo! What brings you into the city this early on a Saturday mornin'?"

Clem and Daniel exchanged a smile. North Tisbury was no city. It had a bakery, a used bookstore, and a roadside vegetable stand.

Bo pointed at a tray of doughnuts on the counter behind

the baker. "Artie, I think we're gonna need about three dozen of those. Cinnamon ones, if they're still warm. And a coupla coffees and a hot chocolate. We're puttin' up a nesting pole today out Long Point way."

"Who's payin' for the pole?" Artie started filling a white bakery box with doughnuts.

"I am—with my achin' back. But we've got a whole bunch of kids from the school comin' out to help. That's what the doughnuts are for. Gonna need some sustenance for a long, cold morning."

"Where's the pole goin'?"

"The old duck huntin' preserve. An anonymous donation from one of our local musical celebrities. You know who I'm talkin' about. He's buildin' a house on some acreage along the shore. Since there's no more huntin' allowed, he says we might as well encourage the birds to come back."

"That's real good, Bo." Artie wound some twine around their three boxes and tied it swiftly. "He does a lot for the Island." Artie grabbed a square of waxed paper and plucked two jelly doughnuts from the display. He handed them to Clem.

She passed a still-warm doughnut to Daniel.

"Thanks, Mr. Caldwell." Clem took a bite. The sweet, yeasty dough melted in her mouth.

The baker smiled. "Just my little contribution in support of your good work."

Bo drove them to the school, where everybody was supposed to meet. Clem spotted Jill's rusty Jeep in the parking lot. Sandy, Joe, and three other kids from science class sat on the school's steps talking to Jill. Everyone wore heavy coats, hats, and gloves. Clem felt grateful for her wool peacoat and thick red mittens.

Bo cut the engine and jumped down. "Mornin', Jill! Everyone here who's gonna be here?"

Jill grinned and looked down at a notebook. "Hmmm, we have seven now. Daniel, Sandy, James, Daisy, Clem, Ryan, Joe . . ."

"Beth said she was coming," Sandy piped up, giving Clem a sympathetic glance.

"Too bad," Clem muttered, only loud enough for Sandy to hear.

Jill checked her wristwatch. "We'll give her just a couple more minutes."

A red pickup roared into the drive and pulled up next to Bo's truck. It was twice as big as Bo's and four times as shiny. The passenger-side door opened and Beth climbed down from the cab. She walked toward them with a sour look on her face.

"Hello, Beth!" Jill called out.

"My stupid mother made me come," Beth muttered.

"Well, I'm glad you're here," Jill said. "Why don't you ride with me? You, too, Ryan, and James. The rest of you kids go in Bo's truck. And hang on tight."

Bo started walking. "Who wants to ride in the cab?"

"I do!" Sandy grabbed Clem's arm and pulled her toward the truck.

They climbed into the cab while Daniel and a few others got in the back. Bo sat in the driver's seat, revved the engine, and put the truck in gear. The sky was just starting to lighten.

At the turnoff for Long Point, a ladder truck from Commonwealth Electric was waiting. The company had donated the huge telephone pole strapped to the top of the truck. Bo gestured to the driver and turned down the dirt road, followed by Jill in her Jeep. The electric company truck rumbled behind them.

They bumped over about two miles of dirt road through the scrub oak forest. After a while, the trees thinned. Beyond the trees, Clem saw clumps of tall beach grass and scraps of blue ocean. Bo parked in a turnout. Everyone piled out and stood around, looking at each other.

"This is the spot," said Bo. "Near here, anyway. Between me, Jill, Fred over there in the truck, and you eight, I think we can carry that pole. It's only about a quarter mile away."

Sandy looked wide-eyed at Clem, raised her eyebrows, and mouthed, "A quarter mile?"

"You've got to be kidding me," said Beth.

Daniel reached into the truck for the doughnuts, took two, and gave Beth the box. "Pass it around," he said. "Sugar helps."

Using a pulley system, Bo and Fred moved the pole from the truck to the ground. Then Bo handed a load of tools to Joe. There was something that looked like two shovels strapped together, plus the largest corkscrew Clem had ever seen, a regular shovel, and a bag of screws and metal braces. He gave Sandy a long board and two thin boards, and handed the nesting platform to Ryan. It was a three-foot-wide square of metal fencing framed by wood.

"The rest of you," he ordered, "spread out along the pole! Put your gloves on!"

The pole was about twenty feet long. Bo took the front end so he could lead. Fred, a tall, burly man in coveralls, took the other end. Clem adjusted her mittens and put her arms around the pole. It was so thick, she could barely get a grip. Most of the others did the same, spacing themselves along the pole. But Beth stepped away, her hands on her hips.

"I'm not gonna rack up my knees carrying that thing," she said. "Are you, Daisy?"

Daisy looked at her, then back at the pole. She hesitated, then walked over to stand by Beth.

"Here then, you carry this!" Sandy shoved the boards at Beth. "I'm gonna help with the pole." She stepped in next to Clem.

Daisy took the tools and bag from Joe. He shrugged and walked over to the pole.

"Heave-ho, everybody!" yelled Bo. "Bend your knees!"

Clem bent her knees and slipped her hands under the pole.

"One, two, three, LIFT!"

Nothing. Clem took a deep breath and tried again. The pole lifted a little. There was a groaning sound from Fred as his end of the pole started to slowly rise. Then Bo's end. Daniel quickly slid his knee underneath the pole to prevent it from dropping back down. Clem copied him. Then she turned her body so she was cradling the pole beside her. She straightened her legs. They had lifted it!

She had no idea if they'd be able to keep it up, though. Already, her back hurt.

"Here we go!" Hugging the pole with both arms, Bo moved toward the water.

The rest of them staggered behind.

"Can't we just roll it?" Clem begged.

"No sirree!" said Bo, huffing a little. "It would flatten everything in its path, including the beach grass. This here grass keeps the beach from eroding away into the ocean. You shouldn't even walk on it, but today we're doing something even more important, so I guess the grass'll forgive us."

They moved slowly. Soon, despite the bitter wind, Clem was sweating under her peacoat. They had passed the trees and were now crossing a meadow of beach grass toward the dunes and the ocean.

Finally Bo gasped, "Awright! This is it!"

Everybody let go.

The pole dropped, scraping Clem's shin on the way down. "Ow!" she yelled.

Daniel was at her side immediately. "Are you all right?"

Clenching her teeth, Clem bent over and pulled up the leg of her jeans. No blood, just an angry red mark on her shin. "I'm okay."

"Daniel," said Bo, "you and Clem go back and get the pastries, wouldja? The rest of you take a breather. After that we got some diggin' to do."

Clem straightened up.

"Are you sure you're okay?" Daniel asked.

The pain had decreased to a dull throb. She nodded. They turned and headed toward the truck.

"Daniel?"

"Hmm."

"Do you think Jill and Bo are—you know—friendly?"

"Of course . . . oh, wait. You mean, more than friendly?"

"Yes." Clem liked thinking of their gentle teacher and the rugged naturalist as a couple.

Daniel looked down but he was smiling. "Maybe. She comes to see him a lot. She's helped with the osprey project. Getting the power company involved and putting up the poles."

Clem knew she was being nosy. But she just couldn't help wondering.

17

No Place Like Home

When they got back with the doughnuts, Bo and Fred were attaching the platform to the top of the pole. They screwed on four metal braces to hold the platform in place. Then they nailed a long board diagonally to the pole and the frame.

"No point getting the birds to lay eggs here on a platform that'll go down the first time it blows," said Bo.

Finally, he nailed two thin boards in the shape of a T to the side of the platform. "That's for perching," he said. "Now let's get digging."

To loosen up the frozen sand and soil, Bo twisted the giant corkscrew into the ground. Then he showed them how to use the clamshell digger—that was the double-shovel tool—to deepen and widen the hole. He jammed it into the ground, then pulled the handles apart to close the shovels around some sand. After he lifted the clamshell digger out of the hole, he dumped the sand.

"Who wants a try?" he said. "We gotta get down at least five feet."

"Me, me!" piped Sandy.

Beth snorted.

Bo handed her the tool, which she took awkwardly and shoved into the sand. Pulling the handles together, she scraped up a clump of sand. On her second try, she did slightly better. Sandy kept at it, wrestling with the digger.

After a few minutes, Clem walked over. "How about I take one side?"

Sandy cast her a grateful look. Together they counted to three and thrust it down into the sand. They got a couple of good scoops, then hit something hard.

"That's dirt," said Bo. "Frozen dirt."

"Time to let the real muscle at it," said Joe.

Sandy straightened and blew her bangs out of her face. "All yours, Rocky."

She grinned at Clem, who was only too happy to stop. They handed him the digger. Joe worked hard for a few minutes, then slowed down, too.

"Not as easy as you thought, huh?" Sandy smirked.

After that, everyone took turns digging—all except Beth, who watched with her arms folded, and Daisy, who did whatever Beth did. After a while, Bo and Fred took over because the hole was now four feet deep and they were the only ones tall enough to keep going.

After another half hour of digging, the hole was finally finished. Bo and Fred made a trip to the truck and returned, huffing and sweating, with a bag of Quikrete instant cement and three long boards. They pushed the boards deep into the hole to form a wall along one side. Then Bo used his hands to dig a shallow ditch leading away from the hole. Daniel started helping him, and then everyone joined in.

Together, they rolled the pole across the sand and laid it in the ditch, with its end pointing to the wall of boards. Bo took a long metal chain and looped it around the top of the pole and the platform. He stretched the chain down the length of the pole and across the hole to the other side.

"Got your gloves on, everybody?" he yelled. "It's the moment of truth! We're gonna have a tug o' war with this here pole."

Daniel walked over, picked up the chain and lifted it to his shoulder, facing away from the hole.

"Really?" said Sandy. "We're going to pull that thing up with a chain?"

"That's the general idea," said Bo.

Clem felt skeptical, too, but she walked over and lifted the chain to her shoulder. Sandy followed, and then the rest of the group joined them. Except Beth, of course.

"C'mon, Beth!" called Jill.

"Nah, that's okay," said Beth. She sat down on a dead tree limb. "Don't worry about me. I'll watch."

Jill picked up the chain, shaking her head. Bo and Fred got ready to pull, too.

"Walk forward," ordered Bo.

Everyone stepped away from the hole, pulling the metal chain taut.

"Get ready to pull. Count of three," said Bo. "One . . . two . . . three!"

They all heaved forward. The pole slid toward them, hit the boards with a jolt, and stopped.

"Keep pulling! Harder!" yelled Bo.

Everybody strained against the chain. The top of the pole rose about a foot off the ground, then stopped. It swayed a little.

"We're doin' it! Keep walkin'!"

Clem tried to step forward, but couldn't move. She felt like she was chained to a rock. Her shoulders ached with all the pulling.

"Don't give up," said Bo. "We don't want to drop it."

"Need a hand?"

Clem looked up to see Beth position herself between Sandy

and Joe and grab the chain. Daisy scurried up behind her and found a spot as well.

"Heave ho!" Beth yelled.

They all leaned into it again. Clem dug her heels into the sand and took a step. The pole began to rise. Step by step, they moved forward across the sand. Clem couldn't see the pole, but she imagined it getting higher and higher. The wood boards groaned loudly as the end of the pole scraped down against them.

Then, suddenly, there was a thump and the chain went slack. Clem looked over her shoulder. The pole stood, tall as a two-story house, in the hole. Joe let out a whoop.

Bo hustled over to the pole and grabbed it. "You kids can let go now. Daniel, give me a hand here. Fred, get the Quikrete. Clem, fetch us some water in that bucket."

Clem grabbed the bucket and ran down the beach. It was a lovely beach, a strip of fine white sand curving in both directions. She stooped at the water's edge to fill the bucket, but could only scoop up about an inch. Taking a deep breath, she tugged off her boots and socks, and rolled up her pants. She stepped into the freezing surf, dipping the bucket quickly. The icy ocean burned and chilled her feet. She shrieked with cold and delight, then ran back barefoot to the others.

Bo had already filled the hole around the pole with the

Quikrete powder. He held a small balance against the pole, making sure it stood straight.

Looking at Clem, he yelled, "Pour!"

She emptied the bucket into the hole. Daniel looked up at her and grinned. She grinned back, feeling happy and silly all at once.

"More water!" yelled Bo.

"I'll do it!" squealed Daisy, peeling off her shoes and socks. She grabbed the bucket and ran down to the water.

Then everyone wanted a turn. They poured bucket after bucket into the hole as Fred mixed the concrete. Soon they were all barefoot and laughing and hopping around to keep warm.

"That's it! We've done it!" yelled Bo, giving the pole a gentle shake and then backing away. He looked up at the platform. "Be it ever so humble, there's no place like home."

18

Merry Christmas

On the day before Christmas, Clem and Nora drove through snow flurries to Nana's house in North Attleborough, Massachusetts. Clem kept wishing that Adam were with them. Every time Nora asked a question or tried to start a conversation, Clem cut her off with a one-word answer. She felt bad about doing that, but she didn't feel like talking.

The snowfall got heavier as they drove farther from the ocean. When they finally pulled into Nana's driveway, an inch of fresh powdery snow covered the lawn.

Nana still lived in the house where Nora grew up, a big old New England house with simple antique furnishings and bare wooden floors. The chairs were tall and straight and the quilts and pillows on the beds were thin and flat from years of use. Nana wasn't poor, but she was frugal. Things had to wear out before she would buy anything new.

Nora said it was because of her mother's New England Puritan background—and because she'd grown up during the Great Depression. Nana's motto was "Use it up, wear it out, make it do, or do without."

They went in without knocking and found Nana standing in the hall.

"Welcome, welcome!" she sang in a high, musical voice. Nana was a little like her house—straight-backed and thin. She always wore her long white hair rolled in a bun at the nape of her neck. Grammy Joe, Clem's other grandmother, liked to smother Clem in hugs. Nana just gave her a kiss on the cheek and a quick squeeze.

But Clem knew there was a lot of love in Nana's bony hug. They had a special bond. When she talked, Nana always listened—unlike Nora. Clem also liked her sharp, dry sense of humor.

Nora gave Nana a peck on the cheek. "Hello, Mother. Merry Christmas. I see you've finally had the spruce and magnolia pruned."

"Yes, dear. They needed it, didn't they?"

"Much better. Better visibility. I'd still like to see you install a convex mirror at the end of the drive so you can see around that curve when you're pulling out, though."

Nora always talked this way with her mother. Business-like and efficient. Clem loved to sit and listen to Nora and Nana's conversations. They used a sort of formal tone, but Clem could hear the affection behind their words.

Dinner that night was quick and casual, even though it was Christmas Eve. Soup and cold cuts. Nana asked Clem questions about school and talked to Nora about her work.

After they finished eating, Nana took Clem's face in her hands. "You are growing like a weed. You need to rest. The blue bedroom is all ready for you."

Clem was tired, and she could tell that Nana and Nora wanted to sit up and talk. She gave Nana a kiss and left to fetch their gifts from her luggage. Clem had wrapped the gifts before leaving the Island. She put them under Nana's Christmas tree.

For Nora, she had a new copy of *Roget's Thesaurus* since her old copy was worn out and leaking pages. For Nana, she had cross-stitched a Christmas tree ornament. Clem had loved the way the cross-stitch patterns came to life as she filled the stiff little squares with brightly-colored yarn. She was pleased with her gifts—but it felt strange not to be putting a present under the tree for Adam.

She woke early the next morning. Her room was dark and cold. Christmas morning always gave her a rich, cozy feeling, but today she felt different—odd and empty and confused. She made her bed quickly, then tiptoed downstairs. The house was silent. Both Nora and Nana were still sleeping.

The Christmas tree had two kinds of decorations—old-fashioned ornaments that had been in the family for a very long time and Clem's own handmade decorations. Nana had saved them all, including Clem's nursery school creations, made from pipe cleaners, Elmer's Glue-All, tongue depressors, and glitter. Clem examined the small pile of wrapped gifts beneath the tree. Most of them were for her. As she straightened, a familiar ornament caught her eye. It was a little framed photo, dangling from a branch. Gently, she unhooked it for a closer look.

There was Nora holding newborn Clem, swaddled in a blanket, Nora's hand cupping her head. Nora was looking down into Clem's tiny face, and baby Clem was looking out at the photographer, who must have been Adam. He had probably made a funny noise to capture her attention. Even though she couldn't see Adam in the picture, Clem knew he was there, with her and Nora. The three of them together.

"What's on your mind, dear?"

Clem turned, startled. She hadn't heard Nana come in. Her grandmother was standing in the doorway in her quilted robe and slippers.

"I'm just remembering how Christmas used to be," Clem said. "When I was small."

"Those were lovely times, weren't they?" said Nana. "You and your mother and father would arrive here at lunchtime, all fresh and rosy-cheeked and laden with gifts. You always brought such a jolly feeling into the house."

That was just how Clem remembered it, too.

"This year seems rather quiet by comparison, doesn't it?"

A lump came up in Clem's throat. She carefully hung the ornament back on the tree, turning her back so her grandmother couldn't see her face. Nana walked over next to Clem and put her arm around her.

"Clementine, your mother has told me about all the time you are spending on your own. I am proud to know that my granddaughter is such a mature young lady. But I also think it is important to remember that part of you is still a child, and you have the right to act like one. Children cry sometimes. And they are permitted to tell their parents what they need."

Clem felt a tear slip down her cheek and she wiped it away with the sleeve of her pajamas. Nana reached into the sleeve of her dressing gown where she kept her tissues and handed one to Clem.

Nana looked thoughtful. "I know you love the Island, but I wonder—would you like to come and spend the second half of the school year here with me? I've got plenty of room, as you know. I'm always here, and the school in town is very good."

Clem stared at Nana, astonished.

Her grandmother smiled. "Just for the next six months or so. Until the school year is over."

Clem wondered if Nora had asked Nana to do this. It didn't seem like something Nana would ask on the spur of the moment. Nana didn't do anything without carefully thinking it over, and she would never ask without talking to Nora first.

So Nora must know. Maybe this is what they talked about last night after Clem went to bed.

Nana waited quietly for an answer. She stood there with her robe belted tightly around her spare frame and her thin wrists poking awkwardly from the sleeves. Clem wrapped her arms around her grandmother and gave her a hug.

"Thank you, Nana," she said. "I'll think about it."

While Nana went into the kitchen to put on the coffee, Clem set out the plates and silverware on the dining room table. Then she sat down in a chair, staring out the window. More snow was falling. The gnarled branches of Nana's apple trees spread like the cracks of a shattered window against the steely sky.

"Merry Christmas!" Nora stood in the doorway, freshly showered. Her wet hair hung in a loose braid in front of her shoulder. "Time to open the gifts!"

"Did you ever climb those trees when you were my age?" Clem asked, turning back to the window.

"Oh, yes. All the time." Nora crossed the room to stand beside her. "See that one there? By the fence? That was the best one. In the summer, I would take a book up there and make myself comfortable in the crook of a branch and read for hours."

That was just what Clem would have done. "Did you ask Nana if I could live here?"

"Oh," said Nora. She pulled up a chair and sat beside Clem. "She told me she might ask you that. No, it wasn't my idea. She seems to think I'm not providing you with enough attention and stability."

"But—I'm fine."

"Are you?"

"I think so."

Nora sighed. "It's hard for me to tell how you're doing, Clem. I'm not even sure if I'm fine, to tell you the truth. This is turning out to be a rough year for me."

"Because of Adam being so far away?"

"Mmm-hmm." Nora's voice squeaked a little.

Clem looked at her searchingly.

Her mother's face was pinched up, like she was struggling not to cry. The thread of anger toward Nora that had been tightening around Clem's heart suddenly snapped. A flood of love for her mother spread warmly through her. She'd been so lost in her own feelings of missing Adam, she had forgotten that it was hard for Nora, too. She stood and hugged her mother. Clem closed her eyes and breathed in the familiar scent of strawberry shampoo and lavender lotion and warm skin, smells that took her back to all the nights she had climbed into the big four-poster bed with Nora and Adam back home in Cambridge.

Clem let go. "Do you want me to stay with Nana? Because I really like it on the Vineyard. I've got some friends there now, so I don't miss Coco so much, and I'm—" she broke off.

"You're what?"

"I want to be there in the spring. To see the ospreys. Do you know about the ospreys? How they fly to South America each winter and then come back to lay their eggs?"

"No." Nora, sat down slowly and gestured toward the other chair. "Tell me."

So Clem did. She hadn't had a long conversation with Nora in weeks, maybe months. Her mother always seemed to be working or sleeping. It felt good to tell her everything at last.

Nora had met Daniel and Bo, but now Clem told her more. She told Nora about finding Quitsa on the beach, and about the hacking tower and seeing Quinn. She told her about Rachel Carson and the DDT and Bo's nesting poles. As she spoke, an idea clicked into place. Clem didn't just love the Vineyard—she wanted to do something to help the Island. She wanted to work with Daniel and Bo to make the Island a better place for the birds, a place they could raise their babies safely. She told this to Nora.

"Then more and more ospreys will come back to the Island every year," Clem finished.

"I can see why you want to stay," said Nora.

"Do you want me to stay?"

Nora took Clem's hand. "To be honest, I do. I would miss you so much. I'm not sure what I would do without you." She smiled, her chin trembling again.

Clem knew this. Nora did need her. Sometimes that was a burden but right now, Clem felt glad. The emptiness and confusion were gone. She felt lighter and clearer, like all the talking had swept away a dark fog inside her head.

China cups rattled as Nana carried in a tray with coffee, milk, and her cranberry-orange muffins. She set the tray down on the dining room table.

"Shall we have a bite to eat before we open our presents?"

Clem smiled at Nora, who reached for her hand.

"Merry Christmas," her mother said.

"Merry Christmas," answered Clem.

19

A Feeling of Safety

January was cold and blustery, but with little snow. Clem went to school all week, then spent the weekend days with Daniel. Every Saturday and Sunday, she would begin the day by making oatmeal or pancakes for herself and Nora, who usually sat at her typewriter, bundled in sweaters. Then she bundled up herself: thermal underwear and jeans, itchy wool socks under her Pro-Keds, a turtleneck, one or two sweaters, and her old wool peacoat plus a cap and mittens.

After phoning Daniel, she would walk her bike out Cobb's Lane to meet him at the main road. Sometimes they headed to Bo's to help out with a project like cage repair or nesting pole maintenance. Other days, they biked to Squibnocket or Lobsterville and explored the town.

One day after a storm, they rode over to Lucy Vincent Beach, where tall cliffs made of clay rose high over the beach.

Daniel showed Clem how to sculpt the multicolored clay right on the face of the cliff. They worked the wet, cold clay until their fingers were numb, making a relief painting of birds and fish. White clay for the gulls, red for the beach, and gray for the rocks and fishes. They didn't notice the rising tide until a wave washed over their feet. Laughing and yelling, they raced back to the parking lot to escape being trapped between the waves and the cliff.

Sometimes they walked the deserted beaches and watched the shorebirds. Until now, Clem had only noticed seagulls and sandpipers at the beach. But Daniel showed her how little she knew. There were loons, goldeneyes, kingfishers, scaup. Mergansers. Sometimes Harlequin ducks. Eiders. Cormorants. Kestrels. Scoters. Even the seagulls came in different varieties. Herring gulls, which she already knew about, but also laughing gulls and ring-billed gulls and black-backed gulls.

So many kinds of birds.

And Daniel knew the names of all of them. At first, Clem didn't understand how he could remember them all, or how he could identify them from far away.

They would be walking along the beach when suddenly he would grab her arm and point.

"What?" She would peer through her binoculars. "I don't see anything."

"Out there between the second rock and the white buoy.

Bobbing on the water. Do you see it? It's a hooded merganser. Look—it's about to take off."

Then she would see it, as the bird flapped and rose above the horizon.

Back at the cottage, Clem thumbed through Adam's *Birds of North America*, looking up the birds they had seen and memorizing their markings and their calls. Soon she could recognize the different sandpipers and plovers by the way they ran along the beach. Some zigzagged, others moved in a straight line. Some bobbed their heads rhythmically. She figured out how to identify birds in flight from the movements and the angle of their wings. She knew that the scaup in Menemsha Creek near Daniel's house fed on tiny crabs, and that the sanderlings on the ocean beach ate the droppings of other birds to get the protein they needed during the winter. Once in a great while, she even spotted a bird before Daniel did. Or maybe he just let her think so.

They didn't see osprey—they were not expected back from Mexico or South America until the middle of March or later. But Clem memorized the osprey silhouette in flight, with a broad wingspan and bent wings. When the ospreys did return, she would recognize them.

Clem finished reading *Silent Spring* and checked out another

Rachel Carson book from the library—*The Sea Around Us*. Rachel Carson had a special way of looking at the beach and its creatures. Size didn't matter. She could make a hermit crab, a shrimp, an eel, or even a strand of seaweed into something amazing and heroic.

Clem also found a biography called *Sea and Earth: The Life of Rachel Carson*. Carson's life was hard. After her father died, she took care of her mother. Then, when her older sister died, she raised her two nieces. Later, she adopted her niece's son. During the Great Depression, Rachel Carson supported her whole family by working as a marine biologist.

Like Daniel, who didn't just love birds but could tell you their names, Rachel Carson knew the name and story of every tiny sea worm buried in the sand. She pointed out that every pinch of sand was made from tiny bits of rock and shells from all over the world. Each grain had been carried by wind and water for thousands or millions of years before ending up on the beach. Clem looked very closely at the sand herself and saw red, white, green, orange, and hardly any boring beige.

Clem was amazed to learn that Rachel Carson never even saw the ocean until she was in college. Then she was hooked.

On second thought, maybe it wasn't so amazing. Clem had spent almost all her life in the city, and she had fallen in love with the sea, too.

Rachel Carson died of cancer at fifty-six, just two years

after *Silent Spring* was published. Her biography didn't say what kind of cancer it was. Clem wondered if the chemicals she wrote about might have made her sick. She wished Rachel Carson had lived to see DDT banned in the US, but that didn't happen until four years ago, at the end of 1972—eight years after she died.

The Island was crisscrossed by a network of old roads and even older footpaths, used by early settlers and maybe the Indians before them. These trails weren't on maps and most visitors to the Vineyard didn't know about them. But Daniel did, and he showed them to Clem. Sometimes they found themselves tromping past signs that said No Trespassing or Private Property. But in the winter, the vacationers and land developers were gone and there was nobody to see them, or care that they were there.

One day in early February, they rode to a spot on North Road not far from Cobb's Lane, left their bikes in the bushes, and followed a path uphill through the young scrub-oak forest to a meadow and a stand of beetlebung trees. Clem had learned from Mr. Willard that these trees were called tupelos by most people. On Martha's Vineyard, though, they had a folk name that dated back to the 1800s, when whale-hunters lived on the Island. The wood of the tupelo was used to make the stoppers for giant casks of whale oil. A cork plug was known as a bung, and the hammer used to pound the cork into the cask was called a beetle. So they called the trees "beetlebungs."

Clem liked knowing these things.

A short climb past the beetlebungs through a grove of scrub oak and patches of blueberry bushes brought Clem and Daniel to the top of Radar Hill, the second highest point on the Island and the site of an abandoned World War II radar tower. When they finally reached the clearing at the top of the hill, Clem gasped at the sudden vista: a vast expanse of blue-green water sparkling in the clear winter sun. Where the water met the smooth, cloudless sky, she could see the Elizabeth Islands, just humps of green at the horizon.

Daniel threw his lanky body down on the dry grass and Clem sat beside him. She took off her hat and tilted her face to the sky to soak up the warm sunshine, then went back to gazing at the view.

"Bo says there are ospreys nesting on Cuttyhunk," said Daniel. Cuttyhunk was the westernmost of the Elizabeth Islands. It was a tiny piece of land with just a few residents. "I've always wanted to go there."

"Why don't you?"

"You have to go by sailboat or motorboat."

"So? There are lots of people who could . . ." Clem stopped, ashamed about forgetting that Daniel was afraid of boats. Anybody would be, if their parents had been lost at sea. "I'm sorry."

"That's all right." Daniel took her hand and gave it a squeeze, then let go.

Clem stole a look at him out of the corner of her eye. He was lying with his chin propped on the other hand, gazing toward the horizon. He looked lost in thought.

"Wouldn't it be great to fly there?" she said, lying back to look up at the sky.

Daniel rolled onto his back and looked up, too.

"In a plane, or on wings?" he asked.

"Wings, of course."

"I would love that."

Their heads were close and their shoulders were touching, just a little. Clem thought it was strange that she should feel so aware of that touch, even though she was bundled up in thermals and sweaters and a wool coat. Even with all that clothing, the connection made her feel as if the blood was moving faster through her body.

She wondered if Daniel felt it, too.

"Do you think Noepe will come back?" she asked.

"Definitely. I mean, I hope she will. A lot of birds die during the migration. But if they make it back, they almost always return to the same nesting place."

"Do you think she'll find a new husband?"

"I hope so. I'm counting on Noepe to raise another family here. We want to keep the osprey population growing."

"I think she'll come back, too."

They were silent again. Clem thought about Adam. He was sort of like a migrant bird.

"Do you think about your parents a lot?" she asked.

"I used to," said Daniel, still looking at the sky. "All the time. I pretended that they were just lost. And they would just chug back into the harbor one day. But now I know they're not coming back."

"Do you remember them?" She had wanted to ask about his parents for so long. Lying side by side made it easier.

"Not well," Daniel answered haltingly. "I was very small when they died. I have some pictures. When I think about my mother and father now, I'm not certain whether I'm really remembering them or just the photographs. But I remember a feeling," he said, turning toward her.

Clem turned, too. His blue eyes were so sad and so trusting. "What was the feeling?"

"It was . . ." He lay back again and sighed. "It was a feeling of safety. I remember that I felt safe once."

Clem remembered that feeling. "You don't feel safe now?"

"It's . . . I don't feel like anything particularly bad is going to happen to me, if that's what you're wondering. It's more like—not feeling really connected to anyone."

"Your grandfather?"

"Well, yes, I love him. But it's different. I can't talk to him about my parents, for example. It upsets him too much. He is not really so strong."

Daniel was even more alone than she was. At least Clem's parents were still alive, and she could still remember what it was like to lie between them under a pile of old quilts and feel the warmth of their bodies. A tear slipped out of the corner of her eye and rolled back toward her ear.

"I miss my father," she said. "I know it's not like having him die, and I probably shouldn't complain to you."

"That's okay," said Daniel.

"But he's so far away. And I'm not sure he's coming back." Clem had never shared this fear with Daniel—or with anyone.

"I was wondering about that," he said.

Clem's eyes blurred with tears. "I'm afraid that he and Nora might be . . . splitting up."

"That must be very hard." Daniel said softly. He reached out with one arm and she moved toward him. He wrapped his arm around her shoulder and pulled her close.

She laid her head on Daniel's shoulder. His old canvas jacket smelled of wood smoke and felt soft against her cheek. She let the tears come.

20

Anyone Like You

On a bright Sunday in mid-February, Clem decided to prune the climbing rose on the split-rail fence along the driveway. Last summer, Adam had taught her to cut the stems at an angle just above a bud eye that pointed in the direction you wanted the plant to grow. She'd almost finished when Daniel walked up the drive, wheeling his bicycle beside him. He leaned the bike against a tree, took off his backpack, and pulled out a package.

"I brought you something," he said, holding it out.

The oddly-shaped parcel was wrapped in brown paper and tied with string.

"A present?" Clem got a tingly feeling. "What for? My birthday's not till March."

"Yes, but . . ." Daniel's words trailed off. His cheeks turned pinker. "Just open it!"

Clem pulled off her gardening gloves and took the package. It was very light. She untied the string and pulled back the paper. Inside was a piece of wood—driftwood, she could tell, but smooth and polished. She stroked it with a finger. Maybe it had been part of a tree root. You could still see the burls and the grain of the wood under the silky surface. It was long and flat, like a boomerang, although not quite as bent or as symmetrical. On the top was a screw hook, with a length of fishing cord attached.

"Hold it by the string," said Daniel.

Clem unwound the cord and let the driftwood dangle from her hand, and right away she saw what it was meant to be: a bird in flight.

"It's beautiful!"

"It's not an osprey," said Daniel. "The wings are too straight. Maybe a herring gull. That's the wood's natural shape—I didn't change it at all. I found it on the beach at Squibnocket, and I thought of you."

Clem smiled at him.

"How did you get it so smooth and shiny?"

"Sandpaper and beeswax," Daniel said proudly.

"I love it," said Clem. She picked up the paper from where she had dropped it on the ground, and noticed a card sticking out.

"You can read that later," Daniel said quickly.

But Clem was already opening the plain white card. She knew his handwriting, careful and neat and slightly tilted.

Dear Clementine,
I've never known anyone like you before.
Thank you for being my friend.
Sincerely,
Daniel

Clem read it twice. Only Daniel would write such a brief, reserved note. But she knew that those few words carried a lot of feeling.

She looked up from the card. Daniel shifted from foot to foot. He had taken off his cap and held it in front of him, gripped in both hands. He looked at her intently, nearly squinting. The blue of his eyes seemed to have grown darker.

"Thank you," she said.

They stood looking at each other as Clem tried to think what to say next.

Finally, he stuffed his hat in his pocket and bent to gather the rose branches Clem had cut.

"Careful! Thorns!" she blurted.

As Daniel gathered the twigs into his arms, Clem didn't move. She wanted him to stop and look at her that way again. Like she was the most important person in the world.

That's when she remembered today's date—February 14.

It was a valentine.

"Oh!" she said.

Daniel straightened up and glanced over. "Are you okay?"

"Yes."

Clem tucked the parcel and card under her arm. She walked over to the fence and found a perfectly dried rose, still on the bush. She clipped it and handed the rose to Daniel, giving him her warmest smile. And he smiled back.

He carefully tucked the rose into his pocket. "I've got something else I want to show you . . . Quitsa's nest."

"Really?" Clem had wondered where it was.

"We need to make sure the pole is in good shape so for Noepe when she returns in March."

"I thought maybe you didn't want to go back to Quitsa's home," said Clem. "That maybe it would make you too sad."

Daniel nodded. "I did feel that way for a while. But now, I think it's time."

"I'll be right back."

Clem ran into the house and put her gift on the table. "I'm going for a walk," she yelled to Nora as the door slammed behind her. She headed toward the shed for her bicycle.

"Never mind your bike." Daniel waved a hand. "You won't need it."

Confused, Clem followed Daniel down the driveway and

onto Cobb's Lane. Turning right would take them toward the main road. Instead, Daniel turned left.

Clem caught up with him. "Quitsa's nest is here? Down my road?"

"Remember where you found him?" Daniel looked amused. "He was on the north shore. The beach isn't far from here if you know the shortcut."

After they walked about a half mile down Cobb's Lane, Daniel turned near a big rock and headed into the woods. Clem could see a faint path in the thick brush. In a minute, they reached a tumbledown stone wall that ran across the path. Daniel scrambled over the rocks, then turned and reached toward Clem.

She took his hand, and he helped her over the wall. After she dropped down to the other side, Daniel kept holding her hand as they walked. It felt like magic. Like their hands had become joined and a ribbon of warmth had traveled up her arm and wrapped around the two of them. Clem looked down at her hand and was a little surprised it wasn't glowing.

They walked on like that for a while until the path sloped downward, and she saw open sky just ahead. That meant they were near the water.

They stepped out into a clearing where the woods surrounded them on three sides. On the fourth side was a steep drop to the ocean. At the far side of the clearing, just before the drop-off, was a nesting platform. Clem could see a huge nest atop the pole, silhouetted against the gray sky.

It was a wonderful spot for an osprey nest, and it was Quitsa's. Right at the end of Clem's road.

She looked at Daniel, and his eyes were sparkling.

They walked to the nesting platform. Daniel let go of her hand then so he could put both his hands on the pole. He tried to shake it. Clem went around to the other side and did the same. This pole looked just like the one they had installed with the class at Long Point, and it seemed solid.

Daniel came around to stand beside her, and Clem could feel something about to happen. He took her hand again and leaned toward her ever so slightly. Her stomach did a flip. Was he about to kiss her? She raised her face, gazing up at him. He leaned closer.

Then his head jerked and suddenly Daniel was looking past her, into the distance, eyes wide with surprise. His face crumpled into an angry frown. Clem turned to follow his glance. At the far end of the clearing where the woods met the meadow, she saw a gap in the trees and a dark patch of bare earth.

Daniel let go of Clem's hand and sprinted toward the patch of earth. Clem ran after him. He stopped short at the edge of the torn-up ground. Someone had been digging. Deep, wide tracks, from a truck or some kind of heavy equipment, grooved the mud. A rutted strip of dirt led away from the clearing.

Brush, cut logs, and uprooted shrubs were haphazardly stacked beside the strip of dirt.

Someone had started building a road.

"I don't believe it!" Daniel kicked a big clod of earth. Fists at his sides, he marched down the strip of dirt.

Clem followed, zigzagging to avoid the muddy spots. Just around the bend, the dirt strip connected with a road. It probably wound right back to Cobb's Lane. And there, where the new driveway met the road, stood a green metal box.

"I just don't believe it," Daniel repeated. His voice was low but filled with rage. "We were supposed to have another year!" His cheeks, already pink from the cold, turned red.

The waist-high green box was the size of a bedside stand. A metal plate with a long series of numbers and letters was attached to the front. And the box hummed.

"What is it?" Clem asked.

"A utility box. They've already run electric to the site. You can hear it."

"Who?"

"The owner, I guess," Daniel said. "He told Bo he wouldn't build on this property for another year at least. But it looks like he's a liar."

"Will he take down Noepe's nesting pole?"

Daniel shook his head slowly. "I have no idea."

21

Thank You for Your Interest

As soon as Clem and Daniel told Bo what they had seen, he called the friend who gave him permission to put up a nesting platform on the property.

Clem and Daniel made cocoa while Bo talked. Clem kept stealing looks at Daniel. His mood had entirely changed. The spark between them, the valentine, the holding hands, the almost-kiss—all seemed forgotten.

Bo hung up the phone and sat down at the kitchen table. "It's bad news." He looked first at Daniel, then at Clem. "He says he got laid off from his job a few months ago. Hadda sell the property just to keep from going broke." Bo shook his head slowly. "I can't believe he didn't tell me. Guess he just felt real bad and couldn't face me."

Bo's friend said the new owner was planning to build a house on the land right away.

"It's a good thing you kids went out there," he said. "Woulda been ten times worse if Noepe came back and laid eggs and then construction started. We gotta take out that pole before the birds come back."

"But that's her pole." Daniel stared at Bo.

"I know, I know. But you know as well as I do that we can't let Noepe nest there. It'll be no good. Big trucks, backhoes, power saws . . . it'll drive the birds crazy. She might even quit the nest."

"Can we stop them from building?" asked Clem.

"Not likely," said Bo. "That's a prime piece of land. Worth more'n a hundred thousand dollars if it's worth a penny. If somebody wants a house there, he's probably not gonna just sit on his hands so our birds can be safe."

"Can we move the platform somewhere nearby?" Daniel asked him.

"Well . . . maybe. But I don't know where. And time's short. Noepe'll find somethin', though. If not on the Island, then she'll go farther north. To Cape Cod, maybe. Or New Hampshire."

"New Hampshire?" Daniel looked Clem.

She knew exactly what he was thinking. Martha's Vineyard was Noepe's home. She deserved to raise her family here.

That nesting pole needed to stay.

Clem and Daniel rode their bikes to the Chilmark Town Hall right after school on Monday. They needed the name of the person who bought the property with Noepe's nesting pole. They described the location of the land, and the clerk pulled out a file.

"Here's the new owner," she said, turning the file around so they could read it.

Clem pulled a notebook out of her backpack and wrote down the name "Emily Brewster."

"I know that name," Daniel said.

"I'm sure you do," said the clerk. "Everybody does, around here. She sells real estate. Her office is just up the street near the post office."

Clem and Daniel crossed the street and walked to the tiny building, less than a block away. The sign above the door read, "EMILY BREWSTER PROPERTIES."

"What are we going to say to her?" Clem asked Daniel as they leaned their bikes up against the weathered gray shingles of the building.

"That she can't build there," he said, marching toward the front door.

"No, wait!" Clem caught up and grabbed his arm. "We need a strategy!"

"Strategy?" Daniel said, looking impatient. "Don't you think she will respond to the facts?"

Clem wasn't sure. Daniel expected everyone to be as rational and as thoughtful as he was. But Emily Brewster surely had her own plans.

"May I help you?" A man sat behind a black desk. He looked about college age.

"We need to see Mrs. Brewster," said Daniel. He sounded gruff.

Just beyond the desk was a table with an architect's model of a building on it. It was a perfect miniature, with little sponge-topped trees and a tiny sign that read, "Burger Boy" and looked exactly like the hamburger chain logo. But Martha's Vineyard didn't have any fast-food restaurants.

Daniel reached out to touch the sign and the man sprang out of his chair and stood next to the model. Daniel pulled back his hand.

"Do you have an appointment?"

"No," Clem jumped in. "But it's important."

"Mrs. Brewster is very busy," the man said. "May I ask what this is regarding?"

"It is about her environmental responsib—" Daniel began.

Clem interrupted, "It's about a property she bought. I'm a neighbor. We live on Cobb's Lane . . . and we have some concerns about the construction."

Looking peeved, the young man scanned a blotter-style desk calendar. "I think she has some time a week from next Wednesday."

Daniel stepped forward. "We need to see her now."

"That's not going to be possible."

"We don't mind waiting," said Clem.

The phone on the desk rang. The young man picked it up and listened, then responded, "Two kids—young people. They want to see you about the Cobb's Lane property. They claim to be neighbors. Mmm-hmmm . . ."

He looked at them. "Names?"

"Clementine Harper."

"Daniel Willard."

He spoke into the phone. "Yes—you heard that? Certainly." He hung up. "You may go in."

Mrs. Brewster was older than Clem expected. As old as Nana, at least. She wore a turtleneck and blazer and had short gray hair. A pair of tortoiseshell glasses hung from a chain around her neck. She was seated behind a big wooden desk.

"I'm Emily Brewster," she said. She waved them to two chairs facing the desk.

They sat down.

"What can I do for you, Cobb's Lane resident and—dare I guess—grandson of Bartholomew Willard?"

"You know my grandfather?" said Daniel.

"Oh, yes, of course," she replied. "Doesn't everybody? It's a rather small island."

"Well then, you know how important the environment is to him—and to all of us," said Daniel.

"I certainly do," she said. "Protecting the environment on Martha's Vineyard is a top priority of Emily Brewster Properties. That's why we support the Vineyard Conservation Society each year with a large donation. I am proud and honored to serve on their board of directors."

Daniel's cheeks were pink. "Then why are you planning to build your house right next to an osprey nesting platform?"

Clem felt sure that he was going about this the wrong way, but she didn't know how to stop him—or what she could say that would be better.

"I imagine you are referring to the new-build on Cobb's Lane," said Mrs. Brewster. She didn't seem rattled at all by Daniel's outburst. "It's going to be a state-of-the-art environmentally friendly house! Double-pane glass, passive solar heat, a recycled-water irrigation system. I suspect your grandfather would be proud."

"He would be nothing of the sort!" Daniel sputtered.

Clem jumped in. "The house is not the problem. It's the construction."

Daniel took a deep breath. "Mrs. Brewster," he said, "The house sounds great. But you probably know that ospreys are an endangered species. Construction this spring and summer will disrupt their breeding process."

"Oh, come now," Mrs. Brewster said. "That pole is twenty-five feet up in the air."

"That doesn't matter," Clem said. "They're wild birds. Loud noises and machinery will scare them away."

Mrs. Brewster spread her hands flat on the desk. "Let's be clear, so there is no misunderstanding." She looked at her gleaming, polished nails, then at Clem and Daniel. "Are you asking me not to build on MY property?"

"Yes . . . at least wait until after the nesting season," said Daniel. "The birds will be returning in just a few weeks."

"And the end of the nesting season is?"

"September."

There was a long pause. Mrs. Brewster looked at her nails again.

"Allow me to explain something," she said very slowly. "I purchased that property for a lot of money. I took out loans. And every month, I make payments on those loans. So I lose money every month until I sell that property."

"You aren't going to live there?" Clem asked.

"No. I buy and sell property. You are asking me to stop doing my job. The answer is no."

"Not even for a few months?" Daniel leaned forward.

"Let's see: March, April, May, June, July, August. That makes six months. Half a year." She stood up. She was tiny—shorter than Clem. "I understand. You care about the birds. I like birds, too. But I must make a living. That pole is on my property. You are lucky I haven't taken it down already. If you are concerned about the birds building their nest there, you have my permission to move the pole yourselves."

Grabbing a cane, Mrs. Brewster came around the desk in a stately fashion, then walked past them to stand by the door to her office. "Thank you for your interest. Good day."

22

A Crack in the Wall

Daniel and Clem sat rocking in the chairs on Daniel's porch. It was Wednesday, two days after their meeting with Mrs. Brewster. They were having a warm spell that made Clem think of spring, even though it was still February.

Clem sucked on a Sugar Daddy. Daniel just stared at his. He hadn't even unwrapped it.

"There must be something we can do," he said.

They had spent the past two days trying to figure out how to save the nesting platform on Cobb's Lane. They had talked with Jill. She told them to contact the Vineyard Conservation Society. Clem wasn't sure that would help, since Mrs. Brewster was a member of their board. Nora suggested calling the Audubon Society. After school, Daniel and Clem used the phone at Clem's house—Nora even gave her permission for the long-distance calls. People answered the phone, took down

Clem's phone number, and promised to contact her with more information.

But no one had called back yet. They were running out of time. Bo said the ospreys could start returning by the second week of March. That was only three weeks away.

Daniel picked up the copy of the *Vineyard Gazette*, the Island's newspaper. It only came out once a week on Tuesdays during the winter. Clem knew he liked to read the bird column. She hadn't even known there was a bird column before meeting Daniel. Now she read it each week, too, to find out about the Island's native birds. When the ospreys came back, it would be big news.

"Clementine—look at this." He handed her the *Gazette* and pointed to a page.

She read the headline quickly. "So the ferry prices are going up?"

"No, under that. In the small print."

Under the heading "LEGAL NOTICES" in tiny type, Clem read:

There will be a public hearing Monday, March 15, 1977, at 5:10 p.m. at the Chilmark Town Hall meeting room to act on a petition for a Variance filed by Emily Brewster under Chilmark's Zoning By-Law Article 5 Section 3.6B. The applicant seeks permission to build a home with a footprint that extends into the 10-foot required buffer zone. The proposed construction will take place at 87 Cobb's Lane; Assessors Map 23 Lot 7.9.

"Cobb's Lane!" Clem put down the paper. "That must be the property! But what does it mean?"

"I'm not sure," said Daniel. "But Grandfather will know."

Mr. Willard was in his chair as usual, bundled up in several blankets although he was seated right next to the stove. He looked tired and pale. But he eagerly took the paper from Daniel and squinted at it, then put on his reading glasses.

"So Emily needs a zoning variance." He made a clucking sound with his tongue. "Looks like there might be a small crack in her wall after all. She wants to build her house closer to the edge of the property than the zoning laws permit. She needs the permission of the zoning board of appeals. There will be a hearing. Do you know what that means?"

"We can save the nesting pole?" Daniel asked.

"I don't think you can be certain of that yet, but you can try to stop her from getting this variance. That will certainly slow her down." He smiled and rubbed his hands together. "I'd love to see you two go up against that old hen. She's been doing her best to ruin the Island for the rest of us for a long time. I think you should attend that meeting."

The meeting was on March 15. The same week that the ospreys might return.

23

City Girl

Clem hopped up and down to keep warm as the ferry dock workers lowered the gangplank into place. As soon as they pushed back the heavy metal door, she spotted Coco, the first person off the boat. She looked more fabulous than ever in a new puffy pink parka with her dark hair pulled up into a grown-up looking twist on top of her head. She had started using black mascara.

Clem felt a little embarrassed, standing there in her old peacoat with a missing button. Then she was smothered in Coco's parka.

"Island Girl! You have no idea how much I've missed you! Everything is crazy without you!"

Clem felt a little choked up. She'd almost forgotten Coco's bright energy—how it surrounded her and made her feel more alive. She gripped her best friend tightly and breathed in her familiar floral scent. Love's Baby Soft. Coco wore it every day. When they broke apart, she grabbed Coco's arm and they headed for the car. Clem tossed her suitcase on the front seat next to Nora and then climbed into the back of the Dart with Coco.

"Mrs. Harper, when are you gonna bring my nature girl back to Boston?" Coco asked.

Nora smiled and looked at Coco in the rearview mirror. "Don't worry, Coco. We'll be back before the fall."

At the house, they dumped Coco's stuff on the floor in Clem's room and threw themselves across the bed.

"Cute room," said Coco, looking around. "Could use a little work, though." Propping herself up on an elbow, she looked at the paint-by-numbers beach picture and then turned to Clem, eyebrows raised.

"Yeah, well, I haven't had a chance to talk to my decorator," said Clem.

They both laughed.

They had so much to talk about. Lying there gabbing, Clem felt as if they'd never been apart. Coco was the same: bubbly, sarcastic, opinionated, and exhausting. But she had new stories to share. Bored with freshmen, she'd started hanging out with older boys.

"They're so cool, Clem!" she breathed. "Like a totally different species!" But she'd been grounded three times since

Christmas. "My parents are so lame. I almost couldn't come this week! But my mom changed her mind because she loves you."

Clem laughed. "I miss your mom. She's funny."

"Yeah, hysterical." Coco stuck out her tongue. "But you do need to come back. You're missing out on some seriously cute guys!"

"Anybody new?"

"Well, I didn't tell you about Ricky."

"Ricky . . . You mean Rick Mathews?"

"No. You don't know him. He doesn't go to my school."

"Does he go to private school?"

"No."

"So . . . where does he go?"

"He dropped out."

"Dropped out! How old is he?"

"Seventeen. And don't look so shocked. That's not so old!" Coco turned fifteen next month. "He's cool . . . and creative . . . and gorgeous . . . and he's nice, too. But my parents wouldn't let me see him."

Clem got up and closed the door, then clambered back onto the bed. "What happened?"

"You don't have to be all dramatic about it. It's not a big deal. My parents are just being their usual controlling selves."

Coco told Clem she had met Ricky at a party. He had

shoulder-length dark brown hair and soulful eyes like Jackson Browne, and his jeans fit just right. He didn't like the party any better than Coco did, and he had a car—so they left together.

"We went to that coffee shop at the Fresh Pond Shopping Center, you know, little hole in the wall, open all night. We talked till two in the morning! It was amazing." Coco looked flushed.

Clem had never seen her so excited about a boy.

"He's in a band, and he paints, and he has all these interesting ideas, and he was totally into me! It was like we discovered this little planet, made just for us."

"It's not a problem for you that he's a dropout?"

"He's not a 'dropout.'" Coco sounded scornful. "School just wasn't doing it for him anymore, you know? He said he can learn more on his own. He writes songs, Clem, and he has all these ideas, and he's so sexy . . ." She frowned. "But my parents don't approve."

When her parents learned that Ricky was seventeen and out of school, they told Coco she couldn't see him. So she'd been meeting him secretly after school in Harvard Square. Once she'd even sneaked out with him at night, tiptoeing past the TV room when her parents were watching *M*A*S*H*.

"Coco! What if you got caught?"

Coco looked disdainful. "What are they going to do?

181

Ground me some more? I hate not seeing him at night, Clem. Sometimes I even wonder if he goes out with other girls."

Clem studied her friend's face. "Has anything happened? Have you kissed him?"

"Well, of course I've kissed him! What did you think?"

"I don't know, I just . . ." Sometimes Coco made her feel so young and inexperienced. It made Clem uncomfortable. "Did you . . . do anything else?"

"Clem." Coco looked at her sternly. "You know me better than that."

"Sorry." But Clem wondered. Did she?

"Anyway, what about you?" Coco rolled over. "Tell me what's going on with that Daniel guy."

Suddenly, Clem's budding romance with Daniel—if that's what it was—didn't seem so exciting. "Um, we still hang out."

"I was thinking you would be doing more than that by now!"

Clem felt her cheeks getting hot.

Coco smiled. "Come on, spill! I need details."

"Well . . . okay." Clem sat up. She thought about Daniel. Those long arms and legs that never quite fit in a chair. His floppy blond hair, his wide mouth, that rare smile that made her feel so happy. The blue eyes that changed color with his emotions. The feel of his hand in hers. His clean, Ivory soap smell. Mixed with wool.

Clem smiled. "He's really cute, Coco."

"Yeah? He's tall, right?"

"Really tall, and his eyes are so blue—"

"I remember, you told me! I want to meet him! Have you kissed?"

"No. I thought we were going to once—but he didn't."

"Clem! You're a modern woman, right? You can kiss him, you know."

Clem fiddled with the blanket. "I'm not like you, Coco."

"What's that supposed to mean?" Coco glared.

"Nothing. I didn't mean anything!" Clem nudged her friend. She hadn't meant to be insulting, but it was true. She wasn't like Coco, not when it came to boys, anyway.

Sometimes she wished she was.

Coco was still fixing her hair when Bo and Daniel arrived at eight the next morning. Clem wanted to show her the nesting pole the class had installed. Clem ran out to the truck to ask them to wait.

"Sure thing," said Bo. "Better tell your friend to bundle up. Fog's comin' in."

Back inside, Nora emerged from her room, wrapped in a robe, her hair all pushed to one side of her head. "Off so early?" she yawned.

"Seriously." Coco nodded and zipped up her parka. "I thought this was supposed to be a vacation!"

"Are you going to wear those?" Clem asked, pointing at Coco's bright-white Pumas. "They might get dirty."

"Well, it's either these or my wedges." Coco put her hands on her hips. "You didn't tell me I should pack for the outback. And by the way—what the heck are those?" She pointed at Clem's rubber boots. "You look like you're going off duck hunting."

Coco bent down to look at her reflection in the side of the toaster.

Clem almost tossed out a retort, but she thought better of it. She was excited about introducing Coco and Daniel—her two best friends in the world—and she didn't want anything to spoil it.

"Don't you girls want some breakfast?" asked Nora. She dumped a scoop of coffee into the percolator.

"Thanks, Mrs. Harper, I'm fine."

"We already ate. C'mon, Coco, they're waiting. Bye, Nora!" Clem grabbed Coco's hand and pulled her out of the house.

They ran up to the passenger side of the truck. Daniel opened the door and jumped down.

"You must be the famous Daniel!" said Coco, before Clem even had the chance to make an introduction.

"Yep, that's him," said Bo, leaning across the seat to offer his hand to Coco. "And I'm Bo. At your service. Why don't you ladies ride up here with me?"

Without speaking, Daniel turned around and clambered into the back of the truck.

Coco watched him and then turned and winked at her. "He's not bad," she whispered.

Embarrassed, Clem looked at Daniel to see if he had noticed, but he had already sat down in the truck bed.

When they arrived at Long Point, the fog had begun to roll in, blurring the grasses and the dunes.

"Brrr! It's cold out here!" said Coco, hitching her zipper up to her chin.

"Let's get moving. That'll warm you up," said Bo.

They started toward the beach, Bo and Daniel in front and Clem and Coco behind.

Coco grabbed her arm. "Does he speak?" she whispered.

"Oh, c'mon, Coco. I told you he was shy."

"Shy! That's an understatement!"

The fog was so thick now that Clem could barely see the hunched forms of Daniel and Bo, walking just ahead. They trudged through the wet mist and reached the dunes just as it started to drizzle.

"It's raining," Coco said. "How much farther do we have to walk?" She pulled her puffy parka tighter.

"It's always colder on the beach," said Bo.

"I'm an icicle! And my shoes are getting wrecked!"

"We're almost there!" Clem tried to sound chipper.

They pressed on in silence. It was high tide, so most of the beach was under water. They had to walk in the soft sand near the beach grass, feet sinking with each step. Clem heard Coco huffing with effort. Finally, the pole appeared, taking shape suddenly in the gloom.

They huddled together and looked up. "Can you believe we carried that thing here and put it up ourselves?" Clem asked proudly. She exchanged a smile with Daniel.

Coco studied the bare platform. "Where's the nest?"

"We only installed it a couple of months ago," said Bo. "The ospreys won't be back for a few more weeks."

"They're probably somewhere in Mexico right now," said Daniel.

"Smart birds," said Coco.

For the first time ever, Clem felt like telling Coco to shut up. She looked at Daniel. He gave her a tiny nod, like he was saying, "It's okay."

"Well!" Bo rubbed his hands together and looked from Coco to Clem. "I'm a little chilled myself. We'd better be getting home."

They turned around and began the long trudge back.

24

What's Fun to Do Around Here?

After lunch, Coco and Clem retreated to Clem's room. Coco pulled some magazines out of her suitcase and tossed them on the bed. *Seventeen, Tiger Beat, Mad.* All their favorites. She plopped down on the bed and grabbed the *Mad* with the Bionic Woman and the Six Million Dollar Man on the cover. Clem sat on the floor.

"Seriously, I don't know how you stand it. This place is like Siberia." Coco paged idly through the magazine. "Nothing to do and cold as hell."

Clem picked up *Seventeen* and flipped it open. She showed Coco the page with "Teen Dating Quiz: Do you know how he really feels?" She tossed the magazine aside. "You want a sweater?"

Coco shrugged and turned the page of her *Mad* magazine.

Clem opened *Seventeen* again and pretended to read. She

waited for Coco to say something about Daniel. And waited. Finally she couldn't stand it any longer.

"What did you think about Daniel?"

Coco didn't look up. "I can sort of see why you think he's cute," she said finally. "But he's not exactly Mr. Personality."

"Give it a little time, all right? He's shy, and you're a little . . . intimidating."

"Me? What do you mean?"

"Just . . . he's not the social type, you know?"

"No, I don't know. And I'm going to try and forget you called me intimidating." Coco tossed aside the magazine and lay back. "I am so bored!" She pulled off a sock and looked at her chipped pink polish. "We could paint our nails."

"I don't have any remover," Clem said.

Coco groaned and pulled her sock back on. "There must be some stores on this island! Didn't we drive through a town when you picked me up at the boat?"

Clem wasn't sure that any of the shops that were open in the winter would interest Coco. Still, they had to do something. And she wanted Coco to be happy. "Okay. Tomorrow we go shopping."

Nora agreed to drive them into town. "You girls can do what you like. Just call me from the pay phone at the ferry ticket office when you want me to come get you." She smiled brightly.

They were almost ready to go when there was a knock on the door. Clem ran to get it.

"Daniel!" She was glad Coco hadn't scared him away. "We were just going into town."

"I can come back later," said Daniel.

Clem hesitated. She really wanted Coco and Daniel to like each other. Now she had another chance. "Why don't you come with us?"

"Are you sure that's okay with your friend?" asked Daniel.

Clem grabbed his hand and pulled him inside. "Hey Coco, Daniel's coming."

"Cool," said Coco. But she didn't smile.

When they reached the Dart, Coco said, "I'll let you lovebirds have the back seat." Then she rode in the front with Nora.

Next to Clem, Daniel sat still and silent for the ride to town. He didn't try to hold her hand.

Nora dropped them off at the top of Main Street. They wandered down the road toward the library. Coco kept stopping to peer into the soap- or paper-covered windows of the closed boutiques.

"Looks like there's some good shopping here," she said. "In the summer."

"Bunch of Grapes is open, at least," said Clem. "The bookstore."

"Great! We can check out the record department!" She looked at Clem. "They do have a record department, don't they?"

Clem shook her head.

Coco threw up her arms. "How have you two not died of boredom already?"

"We could go eat," said Clem. "The Black Dog is open."

"The food there is quite good," said Daniel. "It's one of my grandfather's favorites."

"Okay, let's give it a try," said Coco. "Lead the way."

The Black Dog Tavern was a cozy restaurant overlooking the harbor. It had a big fireplace and the walls and heavy beams overhead were covered with sailing memorabilia: quarterboards carved with the names of old schooners, antique photos, tillers, and bits of rope and other nautical things. Clem hoped Coco would like it.

The hostess seated them near the fireplace.

Coco slipped off her pink parka and rubbed her hands together. "Not bad so far. Let's see what they've got to eat." She flipped open the menu.

The waiter walked over. Clem had seen him around town with several other older boys. He was muscular, like a football player. He placed a board with a small loaf of bread on the table.

"Hey, I'm Gray," he said, looking straight at Coco. "What can I get you?"

She glanced up at him. "I don't know yet. But that bread smells amazing."

"Yeah, they just took it out of the oven." Gray smiled at her.

"I've only eaten here once before," said Clem. "What's good, Daniel?"

He looked thoughtful. "The chowder is delicious." He handed his menu to the waiter.

"That sounds good to me." Clem cut a slice of warm bread and handed it to Coco.

"We'll all have chowder," said Coco. She smiled at the waiter, showing all her teeth.

He winked at her, then sauntered away. Clem noticed that Coco watched him as he disappeared into the kitchen.

"So, Daniel." Coco spread butter on her bread. "Clem says you've lived on the Vineyard all your life."

"Yes, I have," said Daniel.

Clem wished he didn't sound so formal.

"What's that like?"

"I'm not sure how to answer that," Daniel said. "I've never lived anywhere else."

"Well, do you like it here?"

"Yes, I do."

There was a pause as Coco waited for Daniel to elaborate.

Gray returned, balancing three bowls of chowder: one in each hand and one resting on his forearm, cradled against his stomach.

Coco continued to look at Daniel. "So, what's fun to do around here?"

"Not much." Gray answered, as he placed a bowl in front of Coco. "You new on the Island?"

"Nope. I'm just visiting." Coco flashed that smile at him again.

"I figured as much," he said, putting a bowl in front of Daniel.

Clem had seen boys talk to Coco this way before. She was very pretty. With her big hoop earrings, her bold makeup, and her wild dark curls, Coco got noticed almost everywhere they went in Boston. But here on Martha's Vineyard—the most casual, dressed-down place in the world—Coco was almost radioactive.

"You're lucky," said Gray. "I can't wait till I graduate and I can get off this rock."

He placed the chowder in front of Clem. "What about you? Do you live here?"

"Um, sort of. Yeah. I moved here last fall."

"Where?"

"Chilmark. Cobb's Lane."

"I know where that is." He reached into the pocket of his black waiter's apron and brought out a handful of cellophane packages of soup crackers. He tossed them in the center of the table, then looked at Coco.

"You guys partiers?"

"Not really," said Clem.

"Of course," said Coco.

Gray raised his eyebrows and looked amused. Coco and Clem looked at each other. Daniel opened a package of crackers and began slowly dropping them into his soup, one by one.

"We're having a party tonight in West Tisbury. Not too far from here." Gray smiled at Coco. "You should come. Enjoy the chowder." He turned, crossed the room, and began clearing a table.

Coco grabbed Clem's arm. "Don't tell me you don't want to go! That guy is seriously cute."

"But Coco, you don't know him. We don't even know how old he is."

"Oh, come on. Please, Clem?" Coco made a little whimpering noise, like a puppy. "For me? I want to have some fun! You've got to admit, Clem, this place is boring. And after all, we're on break. It's not like it's a school night or anything."

Clem looked at Daniel. "What do you think?"

Daniel put down his spoon. "I can't go," he said. "Grandfather needs me to help with some chores tonight. Besides, I'm not sure I'm invited."

"You see, Coco? Daniel can't go."

"So that means we can't go either?"

Clem squirmed a little. "Yes. No. I don't know. Anyway, how would we get there? I can't ask Nora to drive us. What am I going to tell her? 'Hey, Nora, we met some older guy in a restaurant and he wants to party with us?'"

"I bet if we asked Waiter Guy for a ride, he'd pick us up."

Daniel quietly ate his chowder. He looked worried.

Gray walked up to the table and put down another loaf of warm bread. "I don't do this for everyone, but I thought you might like some more."

"Yum," said Coco and gave him a thumbs-up. "So, Gray. What time do you want to pick us up?"

Clem kicked her under the table.

Coco didn't flinch. Gray placed the check on the table and smiled at her. "Meet me on North Road. At the end of Cobb's Lane. Eight o'clock, okay? I don't want to get lost in the woods back there."

"I don't—" Clem began.

Coco cut her off. "Great! See you then."

25

We Have to Go

Huddled in the corner of the sofa, Clem watched Coco chatting with three boys. Two of them were juniors and the third looked even older. Dressed in a gauzy purple peasant blouse, tight jeans, and tall wedges, Coco looked great. She gestured with her hands, opened her mouth wide to laugh, and tossed her hair. All three boys talked loudly and kept their eyes on her.

Clem was trying to be invisible.

The evening seemed like a mistake from the beginning, starting with lying to Nora about where they were going. Coco made her put on lip gloss, which felt sticky and weird.

Sneaking down Cobb's Lane with their flashlights was fun, until Gray's car rounded the curve. It blinded them with its headlights and screeched to a stop. Clem's stomach dropped.

When Gray rolled down the window, Clem saw four boys

inside the car. She started to panic. But Coco was fearless.

"Room for two more?" She opened the back door and climbed in.

Ears pounding, Clem slid in beside her.

Now Clem wished she had done something different. Told them she had a stomachache. Pretended to trip and twist her ankle. Grabbed Coco's hand and run for the woods.

She should have said no to Coco in the restaurant. If she had been braver then, she wouldn't be sitting here now. She kept thinking about the hurt look on Daniel's face when he found out she was going to the party with Coco. Without him.

Jefferson Starship blared on the stereo. Clem didn't know whose house it was, but it was getting trashed. Someone had set up a ping-pong net on the dining room table and two boys and two girls were playing mixed doubles, laughing and knocking over chairs. Kids were sprawled on the stairs, clustered in corners, sitting on the floor. She smelled popcorn and beer and melted cheese and bitter cigarette smoke. A girl banged into the couch and dropped her cup. Cola splashed Clem's legs, soaking the cushion. She felt the wetness seeping into her pants. In a nearby chair, a girl sat in a boy's lap, kissing his neck.

Coco turned as Gray tapped her on the shoulder. He handed her a bottle of beer and Clem watched as Coco raised it to her lips and took a swig. Then, suddenly, Coco was kissing him. Clem didn't want to look, but she couldn't help herself. At first they kissed gently. But soon Gray had his hands on Coco's hips and was pulling her against him. Coco wrapped her arms around his neck.

Clem didn't know what to do.

The couch jolted as someone dropped down beside her.

"Is that your slutty friend?" It was Beth, looking at her with a nasty smile. "Really going at it, aren't they?"

"What do you care?" asked Clem, turning away.

"I don't," said Beth. "But you look like you do."

"No," said Clem. "You're wrong."

"Ohhh-kaaay. Have it your way." She looked around. "Where's Bird Boy?"

Home with his grandfather, Clem thought—probably asleep by now. Or maybe lying awake, staring at the ceiling, wondering why she had been so rude. Or why she had agreed to go to this stupid party. Or why she let Coco decide everything—the way she always did.

Clem had acted like Daniel didn't matter, when really he mattered more than anything.

Gray stopped kissing Coco and grabbed her hand. He led her across the living room and down a dark hallway. He opened a bedroom door and they disappeared inside.

Clem stood up, peeling her wet jeans away from her legs.

Now her hands felt sticky. She turned back to Beth. "Do you know where the phone is?"

"Why?"

"Just tell me!"

Beth's eyes widened. "All right, already! I think it's in the kitchen. Or maybe—"

But Clem was already halfway across the room. In the kitchen, a couple sat on the counter, making out. The phone hung on the wall behind them. Reaching around, she picked up the receiver and dialed her own number.

Nora picked up after just one ring. "Clementine?"

"Hi," Clem said, her hands shaking. "Can you come pick us up?"

During the dark ride here, Clem had paid attention. She gave Nora directions to the house.

Then she walked down the dark hallway to the bedroom door, which was slightly cracked. She pushed it open. In the dim light, Coco and Gray lay on the bed, kissing. Gray slid his hand under Coco's shirt.

Clem flipped on the light. "Excuse me!" she said loudly. "Coco—we have to go!"

"What the hell!" Gray sat up. He squinted in the sudden brightness.

Coco quickly pulled down her shirt and sat up too.

"Clem, what's going on?" She pushed back her wild hair and looked confused.

"Coco. We have to leave. I called Nora and she's going to meet us at the road in ten minutes."

"Why? Is something wrong?"

"What? No. It's just—we shouldn't be here!" She raised her eyebrows and looked at Gray. "It's not a good idea."

Understanding dawned on Coco's face. Her expression changed from confusion to anger. She smacked her forehead and flopped back on the bed.

Gray glared at Clem. "Listen. Your friend's a big girl. She can make her own decisions. You go on home and I'll bring her back later."

Clem took a step toward Gray. "Do you even know her name? And how old she is? Did she tell you she's fourteen?"

Gray's eyes widened. He turned toward Coco. "You said you were sixteen."

"I did not!" Coco sat up. "*You* said I *looked* sixteen."

"Whatever," said Gray. "Maybe you better go home."

"I wish I could." She stared angrily at Clem. "To my home. I hate this island."

Her eyes looked like two black holes. Coco had never looked at Clem like that before. Like she hated her.

They found their coats buried under a pile of others in the entryway. Without talking, they left the house and trudged down the gravel drive to the road. The slender crescent moon offered little light. When they reached the road, Clem sat on a boulder while Coco leaned against a tree. She kept her face turned away from Clem.

"Coco, I—" Clem began.

"Don't even bother," Coco said. "I don't want to hear it."

When Nora finally arrived in the Dart, Coco climbed into the backseat. Clem took the front seat.

"I thought you were going over to Daniel's," said Nora. "What is this place?"

"Somebody's house," said Clem. "We went to a party."

She looked back at Coco. Her mascara had smeared. Clem could see a bluish bruise on her neck. A hickey.

"Oh," said Nora. "And Daniel?"

"He didn't come."

Coco glared at Clem. She pressed her lips together, her jaw tight. She looked like a different person.

"Hmm," said Nora. But she didn't ask any more questions.

Clem was grateful for that.

In the morning, Coco called home. Afterward, she told Nora that she was needed at home and would have to leave. Nora took her to the ferry, and Coco was gone.

Three days early.

26

Speak Up, Miss Harper

Daniel didn't call or stop by all weekend. Clem spent Saturday and Sunday inside, reading. She didn't feel like doing anything else.

When Monday morning came around, Clem hoped that things would be back to normal. But Daniel didn't even look for her on the bus. He just took a seat alone at the front, the way he always had in the days before they became friends.

After school, Clem let him get on first, then sat in front of him. She sat sideways, with her back against the window.

"Hey."

Daniel seemed to shrink back in his seat. "Hi."

"Are you going to go see Bo this week?" she asked.

"No . . . I don't think so," he said.

"Why not?"

"I'm doing research. For the zoning hearing."

"That's good. But isn't Bo helping?"

Daniel shook his head. "He thinks I should drop it. He says it's a lost cause."

"How can he know that? We have to try to save the nest."

Daniel was silent.

"Can I help?"

"That's okay," Daniel mumbled. "You don't need to."

Clem fiddled with the button on her coat and looked away so he wouldn't see how hurt she felt.

"Maybe I'll ask Jill for some advice," she offered.

"Okay," said Daniel. He turned to look out the window. Clem slowly swung her feet to the floor and faced front. He was sitting right behind her, but it felt like he was a million miles away.

"It's a good idea, testifying before the zoning board," said Jill. "Citizen action. But the only experience I have with zoning boards is when my neighbors complained about my chickens. I had five of them, and you're only allowed to have four."

"Did you fight the complaint?"

"When I looked at the zoning regulations I saw that they were right. The law's the law. So I gave away one of my New Hampshire Reds."

"You didn't even go to a hearing?"

Jill shook her head.

"What would you do if you were me?"

"Well . . ." Jill looked out the window thoughtfully. "I'd talk about the nest. Unless Daniel comes up with something really good in his research, your best bet is to appeal to the board's emotions and their sense of duty to the environment."

Clem didn't know if she could stand up and talk in front of Emily Brewster and the board. She felt her heart speed up at the thought of it. "I don't know what I'd say."

"You know, Rachel Carson hated public speaking. Then CBS asked her to tell her story on television. She knew that might get people to pay attention. Rachel was very sick with cancer, but she did it. And the day after the TV show aired, Congress announced that they would investigate pesticides."

Clem felt a little better. If Rachel Carson was brave enough to go on television, then maybe she could be brave enough to speak at the hearing. Clem wondered what Daniel was doing to prepare. It made her sad to realize she had no idea what his plan was.

Nora drove Clem to the town hall for the zoning board hearing. Daniel's bike was leaning against the building, so she knew that he had already gone inside.

In the town hall lobby, they found a sign directing them to

the hearing, up a flight of stairs. Clem had imagined a big courtroom, with the zoning board up front behind a long table, and everyone else sitting on benches. Instead, it was a small room with six people sitting around a fake-wood conference table. One of them was Mrs. Brewster.

Three men and two other women also sat at the table. Each had a packet of papers and a little piece of wood with a brass nameplate. Clem recognized two people. She had seen the tall man in overalls working on the pier at Menemsha, unloading fish from one of the big boats. And she knew Mrs. Abel from the postal counter at the general store. Her nameplate said "Janice Abel, CHAIRPERSON." A small gavel lay on the table beside Mrs. Abel's packet.

One more person, a man who clearly wasn't on the Board, sat on a chair in the corner of the room to Clem's right. He was writing in small notebook.

Daniel sat in a chair by the wall on the left side of the room, studying some papers in his lap. He was wearing a tie and a shirt with a button-down collar, and his hair looked shorter. Clem quickly combed her ponytail with her fingers. She hadn't thought to wear anything special.

Daniel slid the papers he'd been examining into a beat-up leather folder. That was probably his grandfather's, Clem thought. Maybe the tie, too. She wondered why Mr. Willard wasn't here with Daniel. She knew he wanted to see this.

She and Nora walked around the table and sat down by Daniel.

Clem turned to greet him. "Hey, Dan—"

Mrs. Abel cut her off. "Are you here for the zoning hearing?" she asked briskly, looking at Nora.

"Yes," said Daniel and Clem in unison.

"Ah. Well then, let's begin." Mrs. Abel picked up the gavel and tapped it lightly on the table. "This meeting of the Chilmark Zoning Board of Appeals is now in session. For the record, today is the fifteenth of March, nineteen-hundred-and-seventy-seven. All board members are present, as is the applicant, Emily Brewster. We have two citizen petitioners as well. State your names and addresses!"

"Daniel Willard, 18 Coast Guard Drive."

"Clementine Harper, 12 Cobb's Lane." Her voice shook a little.

Mrs. Abel looked down at her packet. "We have an application before us today for a variance related to a buffer zone encroachment pursuant to By-Law Article 5, Section 3.6B. The property address is 87 Cobb's Lane. Emily?"

Mrs. Brewster looked up and cleared her throat. "I believe it's rather pro forma, Madam Chairwoman. We are planning to build a two-story, five-bedroom home on the property. The plan conforms to regulations, except that we would like to locate the northeast corner of the house eight feet from the property line rather than the required ten. This will provide a lovely water view from the second floor of the house. We have spoken with the owners of the abutting properties with homes. No one objects."

Daniel raised his hand.

"Yes, Mr. . . ." Mrs. Abel looked down at her notes. "Mr. Willard?"

"If you please, Madam Chairwoman."

Clem was impressed.

Daniel stood up. "The property next to the corner where Mrs. Brewster wants to build does not have a house. But when the owners of that property do build a house, I think they will find that Mrs. Brewster's building blocks their water view."

"Let's take a look at the map. Page six in your packets," said Mrs. Abel.

The others began flipping pages.

"Madam Chairwoman," said Mrs. Brewster with a tight smile. "All abutting property owners have been notified of my plan. The young man is imagining an objection that doesn't exist. If another property owner were concerned about it, he or she would be here."

"Or they would have sent us a letter or something," said the tall man in overalls. "But we haven't gotten anything."

"Well, then," said Mrs. Abel, looking at Daniel, "this isn't a problem."

Daniel sat down. His shoulders slumped.

"I will entertain a motion for approval," said Mrs. Abel.

"So moved," said a sour-looking man on her left.

"Wait a minute, Janice." The man to her right laid a hand gently on the chairwoman's arm. He was an older man, dressed in a turtleneck and a wool sweater. "I'd like to hear from the young lady." He looked at Clem. "Did you come to raise an objection to this plan, Miss Harper?"

Everyone was looking at her. Slowly, Clem stood up. Her heart was beating fast. She tried to breathe but she felt like she was strangling.

"I don't know how this fits with your zoning laws." Her voice sounded small. "But there is a big problem with Mrs. Brewster's plans for the property."

Mrs. Brewster frowned at her. Clem suddenly noticed that the room felt very warm.

This was it. Her Rachel Carson moment. Her chance to say something in defense of nature. To say something that would matter.

"It's about a nest."

"Speak up, Miss Harper," said Mrs. Abel.

Clem took a deep breath. "I said . . . it's about a nest. An osprey nest."

"Go on."

"There's an osprey nesting platform on the property." Her

voice was a bit louder now. "Daniel—I mean Mr. Willard—built it there, along with Bo Jameson. The previous owner gave them permission. The ospreys were almost extinct a few years ago, because of DDT. You can read about it in a book by Rachel Carson."

Three of the board members nodded.

Clem took another breath. Her words were starting to flow. "Anyway, the government banned DDT in 1972 and Daniel and Bo have been helping the birds by putting up nesting poles. Ospreys come back to the same nesting place every year. Three years ago there were only two pairs of ospreys breeding on the Vineyard, now there are seven. They're coming back!"

Everybody was looking at her now. Mrs. Abel smiled at her.

"The osprey who nested on Mrs. Brewster's property last year is coming back soon. If there's loud construction, she will probably abandon her eggs. Those chicks will never hatch."

Clem sat down.

"Mrs. Brewster," said the older man in the turtleneck and sweater, "Are you aware of this osprey pole?"

"I am," she said. "And I have no intention of taking it down."

"But the construction!" Clem stood up again. "You told us you wouldn't wait!"

"I cannot afford a delay," she said. "But I will do everything in my power to protect your nest."

"That won't matter." Daniel stood up. "Miss Harper is right. With all the activity and noise, the osprey won't stay on her nest."

Mrs. Abel smiled at them again, this time with pity. "I understand your concerns, my dears, but they don't have anything to do with zoning laws. Perhaps you can find another way to help these birds. There is a motion to approve, and a second. All in favor?"

"Aye," said the man on her left.

"Aye," said Mrs. Abel.

"Aye," said the other woman.

The older man hesitated, then said, "Aye."

It was over. They had lost.

Clem turned to look at Daniel, but he was already on his way out the door.

She jumped up, glancing at Nora. Her mother nodded, motioning with her hand as if to say, "Go on!" and Clem rushed after him.

But Daniel didn't slow down, or even look back. He ran out of the building, jumped on his bike, and took off. It was already dark. Within a few seconds, he was out of sight.

Clem slumped onto a bench, staring at the dark spot in the road where Daniel had disappeared. Nora, who had followed her out, sat down beside her and put her arm around Clem's shoulder.

"I'm so sorry, Clem."

"I don't understand! It's like they didn't even hear us!"

"I don't understand, either. You were terrific in there."

"But it didn't make a bit of difference."

"Well, it did to me. You made me very proud."

Clem leaned her head on Nora's shoulder. She knew that her mother's words should have made her feel good—or at least a little better. But she missed Daniel. She wished he was sitting next to her on this bench right now.

And Mrs. Brewster was still going to build that house.

27

Unbelievable

"You know what we used to do when we wanted to change something, Sunshine?"

Clem could hear Adam getting excited, 835 miles away in Ohio.

"Protest. We protested about Vietnam and civil rights and women's rights. We had marches. And sit-ins. You should make a big noise. Ruffle people's feathers!" Adam chuckled. "Feathers . . . get it?"

Clem had gone to marches with Adam and Nora when she was little. People carried big, hand-painted signs and sang and chanted. Most of the time, she just saw people's legs. Jeans and sandals and sneakers and even bare feet. Clem remembered feeling scared. She always held tightly to their hands.

"You think we should have a protest march?"

"Yes! Make a show of strength!"

"There's not very many of us."

"You've already made a great start by testifying before the zoning board. Now get your friends. Have a picket line outside her office. That'll make the news! That'll fix Mrs. Brewster. Businesses hate bad publicity."

Clem thought about it. She didn't know if Daniel would like this idea. She would be embarrassed to ask Sandy and the other kids who had helped with the pole at Long Point. They might think it was silly. Maybe it was silly.

"I could ask my teacher about it," said Clem.

"No grown-ups!" said Adam. "Kid power!"

After she got off the phone with Adam, Clem sat down at the kitchen table and made some fliers.

SAVE THE OSPREYS!
Rally in front of Emily Brewster Properties
State Road, Chilmark
March 21, 4:30 p.m.
BRING SIGNS!

If she were in Cambridge, she would just make one flier and then print copies at Kinko's, but that was not an option here. So Clem wrote it out twelve times by hand—one for each kid in her science class.

She made one for Daniel, too.

The next day at lunch time, Clem handed out the fliers. She went to Sandy first. She was sitting at a picnic table with a girl named Debbie. Sandy took the paper and cocked her head, studying it.

"Why Emily Brewster Properties?" she asked.

"She wants to build a house on a nesting site. The birds will be back in a few weeks and the construction will scare them away."

Sandy folded the paper and put it in her pocket. "I don't know, Clem. I'll think about it."

"Thanks." Clem handed a flier to Debbie. She walked over to Missy and Joanna. They took the papers from her without comment.

"Do you think you can come?" Clem asked.

"I dunno," said Missy, one of the quieter kids in the class.

"It would make a big difference," urged Clem. "Maybe we'd even be in the newspaper!"

"I'm kinda busy after school," said Joanna. "I have to help my folks out down at the barn."

"Well, think about it, okay?" Clem lifted her chin, trying to look cheerful.

Beth was next. Clem dreaded talking to her, but she knew

that Beth had the power to influence the others. She walked over to Beth and Daisy.

"Whatcha want, Washashore?"

Clem held out the paper.

"What's that?" She didn't take it. Didn't even look at it.

"It's a flier." Clem jiggled it a little. Beth still didn't take it.

"A flier. Huh."

"We're going to have a protest. To help save one of the osprey nests."

Beth looked at Daisy. "What'll they think of next, huh, Daze? A protest."

"To save a nest. Like the one we built, remember?"

"Gimme that." Beth snatched the flier.

"'Rally in front of Emily Brewster Properties.'" She read it out loud in a mocking tone. "Emily Brewster Properties? There's no nest there! You don't even know what you're talking about, Washashore."

"The nest is on land she bought on Cobb's Lane." Clem tried to sound calm. "She wants to build a house there, right now. We want her to wait until fall, after the ospreys raise their chicks."

Beth stared down at the flier, shaking her head. "Unbelievable," she said.

For a wonderful moment, Clem thought she was convinced. Then Beth stood up. Kids turned their heads to look.

"Unbelievable," she repeated. "You come here from off-island. You've been here, what? Six months? And now you think you know what's best for the Island? You want to protest against a local business lady because she wants to build a house on her own land?"

Clem took a step back from Beth. Some of the kids had moved closer. Clem saw Daniel standing at the edge of the circle.

"You don't know what you're getting into, Washashore." Beth stepped toward Clem. She narrowed her eyes and sneered. "You don't know anything. Emily Brewster is a Vineyarder! Her family worked hard to make this island what it is. Just like mine! Did you know that Emily Brewster is Sandy's grandmother?"

Clem shook her head.

"You know why you didn't know? Because you're not from here." She crumpled the flier and flung it down in front of Clem. "That's what I think of your protest."

Beth turned and walked back into the school, with Daisy following. Joanna and Missy left, too, dropping their fliers on the table.

Clem slumped onto the bench with her back to the picnic table. So much for her protest.

Daniel sat down beside her.

She didn't want to look at him. She felt like an idiot.

"That was a good idea, Clementine." Daniel said softly.

Clem bit her lip. She refused to cry in front of everybody.

"Maybe Beth is right," said Daniel. "Maybe we should leave Mrs. Brewster alone."

Clem looked at him in astonishment. "Are you kidding?"

"No." Daniel looked serious. "Beth has a point. Emily Brewster is important. She's rich and knows everybody here. We're only teenagers—and you're new here. Maybe that shouldn't matter, but to a lot of people, it does. We can't make her change her mind. We'd be wasting our time."

Suddenly Clem felt angry. "What does it matter that I'm new here? Why didn't you stick up for me?"

"I'm sorry," he said. "I think Beth might be right."

"Right about what?"

"About Emily Brewster having the right to build on her own property."

"Really?" Clem got up from the bench and stood in front of Daniel. "What about Noepe's right? She was there first! So you're ready to just give up? Just quit?"

"I don't want to quit. I'm being realistic."

The bell rang. Clem turned toward the school.

"Clementine, I think we should focus on relocating the nest instead."

But Clem didn't want to relocate the nest. She wanted it to

stay right where it was, so Noepe could find it and start a new family. She didn't want Noepe to lose everything.

"Forget it, then." Clem stood up and turned away from Daniel. "It's over."

"Clem." He sounded hurt.

Even as she started walking away, Clem wanted to take her words back. But she felt hurt, too. She kept on walking.

As soon as she got home that afternoon, Clem called Adam. He picked up after the first ring.

"I miss you so much," she whispered. "Why can't you just come back? Or at least visit? I hate it here without you."

"I miss you, too, Sunshine. I love you more than anything. But I'm starting a new quarter and I have a whole new batch of students to get to know."

Clem didn't want to hear about Adam's students. "You could come for just a weekend."

"I need to be here, Clem. To show them I'm serious. They're considering me for a permanent position here. No guarantees, but I'm feeling hopeful."

"So you need to stay in Ohio?"

"Yes. And Kate tells me that the university press is about to offer me a publishing contract."

"Kate? Who's Kate?"

"Someone I've gotten to know here. She's the poetry editor. Things may finally be coming together for me."

Coming together. Clem wondered what that meant. Where she was, things were coming apart.

She gripped the phone tighter.

"I think summer would be the perfect time for you to visit," said Adam. "We could go camping. I can show you around the campus."

"You mean you're not coming back for the summer?"

"Well," he said slowly, "I might have to teach."

"Would Nora come to Ohio, too?" Clem's voice cracked a little.

Adam paused. "That's up to her."

28

Are You Awake Now?

That night, Clem dreamed she was paddling a canoe in Menemsha Pond. A thunderstorm rolled in. The sky darkened and the wind whipped up. She turned the canoe around and headed toward shore. Then she heard a loud squawking. There was a big nest on a rock jutting from the water. An enormous herring gull stood at the edge of the nest, its wings outspread.

"*Awk! Awk! Awk!*" it called.

Then Clem heard something else—tiny peeps. There were baby gulls in the nest.

Clem paddled closer. The gull leapt onto the prow of her canoe and stared straight at her.

She pulled the canoe alongside the rock and looked into the nest. Three tiny seagull chicks stretched their thin necks. They were so young that they didn't have feathers. They looked more like lizards than birds.

She scooped one up and placed it in the bottom of the boat. Then a wave hit the canoe and it rocked violently. Clem nearly fell out. Then another wave hit her. The canoe pitched again.

The mother bird squawked louder. She was begging Clem to keep trying. Clem reached out for another chick when a third wave came toward her. The wave was so high, she was afraid it would overturn the canoe. She put her hands in front of her face—

And awoke to find Nora looking down at her. Clem's heart beat so fast that it hurt.

Nora sat down next on the bed. "Clem, honey? Are you awake now?"

"I—I guess."

"You were having a nightmare. You screamed. Are you all right?"

Clem nodded. Nora stroked her hair gently. Just like she used to do when Clem was small. It felt good.

After about five minutes, Nora asked, "Better now?"

"I think so."

Nora kissed her on the forehead and went out.

But Clem couldn't sleep. She tossed and shifted the pillows. She kept thinking about her dream. The baby gulls represented the ospreys, of course. Or did they?

Finally, she got up. Her digital clock read 5:47 a.m.

She went to the bathroom, washed her face, put on deodorant, and got dressed. Then she laced up her L.L.Bean boots and grabbed her school backpack from her room.

Clem jotted a quick note and left it on the table: *"Went for a walk. I'll probably go straight to school after. See you tomorrow. XOXO Clem."*

When she stepped softly onto the front porch, the darkness was beginning to thin. She got her bike out of the shed and headed toward Menemsha.

The water of the Vineyard Sound was silvery and calm. The sun rose on the other side of the Island, the eastern side. Here, on the northwest side, the day sneaked in. A haze lay over the Sound, blurring the edge between the water and the smooth gray sky. The pebbles lining the shore clacked softly as gentle waves washed over them.

Clem walked along the beach, sorting her thoughts like small stones.

Adam wanted her to visit this summer. She remembered when he left last summer and she had begged him to take her. But now she didn't want to spend the summer in Ohio.

She wanted to stay right here on the Island. Or go back to Cambridge like they'd planned, where the Vineyard was just a drive or a bus ride away.

Being on the Island had changed her.

She had testified before the zoning board. She made her own dinners and went places on her bicycle and helped Bo with the nesting poles. She knew about Rachel Carson. And she had met Daniel.

This year on Martha's Vineyard was supposed to be a waiting year. Waiting for her parents to figure out their jobs. Waiting for her family to come back together. Waiting for everything to get back to normal.

But it didn't feel like a waiting year right now. It felt like she was standing on the edge of a nest, almost ready to jump.

She tilted her head back to let the rising breeze fan her hair. It was almost sunrise. Pink spread along the horizon like watercolor on wet paper. The sky overhead had gone from gray to blue. Against that sky, she saw a bird—an enormous bird, black and white. Its striped wings ended in four long feathers, like outstretched fingers. Dark circles marked the elbows of its outstretched wings.

It was an osprey.

Clem started to run after the gliding bird. She squinted. Was it Quinn? No, it couldn't be. Daniel had said Quinn would stay away a full year before returning to breed. Noepe? She didn't know. How could you tell one osprey from another, anyway? Clem hoped it was Noepe—and she hoped it wasn't. They weren't ready!

Maybe she could see if the bird was banded. But the bird's legs were tucked up. Even as Clem ran faster, the osprey flew farther and farther away. Finally, she had to give up. The bird became a small dot in the sky. Then it disappeared.

Clem stopped running and fell to her knees in the sand.

Exhausted.

And exhilarated. An osprey!

29

No Answer

"Daniel!" Clem banged on the door of the old house.

It was almost seven thirty now and the sun was up. Everything looked sharp and crisp in the clear, cold light. Clem couldn't wait to tell him what she had seen. All the misunderstandings between them would disappear. Daniel would grab his binoculars and they would go down to the beach together and look for the osprey.

Daniel would know if it was Noepe. She might even have found a new mate already. Maybe they would have to get Bo so they could take down the pole today.

She knocked again and peeked through a window. The reading chair light was on, but the room was empty. Maybe Daniel went out early for a walk. Mr. Willard might still be sleeping. He hadn't been feeling well lately.

Clem waited another minute or so on the porch, then went

back down the path toward the Coast Guard station. She walked to the bus stop and waited for Daniel.

He didn't show up. When the bus came, she got on alone. She sat by a window near the front and stared out. Nobody would sit with her if she didn't look at them as they walked past. Clem wanted to be alone.

Maybe Daniel had already spotted the osprey himself. Maybe he and Bo were moving the pole right now. Clem hoped this wasn't true.

All day long, Clem looked for Daniel in the hallways and in class. He never appeared.

During science class, Sandy turned around in her seat and looked at Clem. "Where's Daniel? He never misses school."

"Maybe he's sick."

Sandy narrowed her eyes. "I thought you two were . . . friends." She made quotation marks in the air with her fingers.

Clem shook her head. "I don't know where he is."

She was first in line for the bus that afternoon. She ignored her stop and rode all the way to Daniel's stop in Menemsha. As she walked across the marsh, she noticed that the rusty old car was gone. Was it gone this morning? She didn't remember. The car was so old and broken down that she'd never thought it might still run.

Clem knocked but there was no answer. She opened the door and walked in.

Inside, the lights were still on but the house was chilly. Clem could still smell the familiar aroma of apples and tobacco, now mixed with the smoky smell of ash. The fire had gone out.

She put her hand against the glass of the wood stove. It was cold. Daniel and his grandfather never let the fire go out.

"Daniel? Mr. Willard?"

The house was utterly still.

Clem had never gone farther into the house than the living room where she and Daniel spent so many cozy afternoons. Now she tiptoed into the hall, where she saw two closed doors. She went to the first and turned the knob.

The door swung open with a creak. Clem knew right away it was Daniel's room, because his school bag was on a chair in the corner. The bed was unmade. She could see the impression of Daniel's head on the pillow. She had an impulse to go and touch it but she didn't.

Clem saw a desk against the wall with a row of books held up by bookends, their spines neatly aligned. On a bureau was a framed photo of a smiling couple standing on the Menemsha fishing docks.

Daniel's parents.

She walked over to get a closer look and tripped over a lump of clothing. Daniel's pajamas, lying in a tangle on the floor.

Clem shivered in the cold room. Something was wrong. Daniel was always so deliberate and careful. He wasn't the kind of person who left clothes on the floor and didn't make his bed.

She went down the hall to the second room. Stepping inside, she smelled pipe tobacco. She recognized Mr. Willard's red slippers, lined up beside the bed. Just like Daniel's, the room was spare and mostly tidy.

But the bedcovers were thrown back and a chair had been knocked over.

Daniel and his grandfather must have left in a hurry, maybe in the middle of the night. Maybe Mr. Willard was sick. He hadn't been feeling well lately.

The car was gone. If they had driven to the hospital, Clem could find them. There was only one hospital on the Island.

Clem grabbed her backpack and rushed out of the house and down the road. She would call Nora from the pay phone at Seward's Market and ask for a ride. Then she remembered. Nora had left this morning to teach in Boston. She wouldn't be back until tomorrow.

When she reached the store, a truck was starting up in the Home Port Restaurant parking lot across the street. Clem knew she wasn't supposed to hitch, but this was an emergency.

She stuck out her thumb.

"Willard? Let me see." The emergency room receptionist thumbed through a binder on the counter. "I just got here an hour ago. What time did you say he was admitted?"

"I don't know," Clem said. "Sometime during the night." She had seen the rusty car in the hospital's parking lot, so she knew Daniel and Mr. Willard were here.

"Here we go," said the receptionist. "Bartholomew Willard. Looks like he came and went."

"What do you mean?" Clem demanded. "His car is here."

"That's because they sent him to Massachusetts General in Boston. In the 'copter."

"Helicopter?"

"Yup. Fastest way to get there."

"And his grandson went with him?"

She shook her head. "Not on the 'copter. They don't allow any passengers."

Clem knew Daniel wouldn't want to leave his grandfather alone. He would have figured out a way to get to Boston, too.

"What's wrong with Mr. Willard?" she asked.

"Doesn't say. Are you family?"

Clem shook her head slowly and backed away. If the doctors had made Mr. Willard fly to Boston, something terrible had happened to him. She felt sick to her stomach.

Then she thought about Daniel, all alone at the hospital. He didn't have any family or friends to go to or to call for help. If Mr. Willard was seriously ill, or worse, Daniel might have to go and live somewhere else. He might have to go into foster care. Maybe even leave the Island.

She was thinking too far ahead. But Clem knew that she wanted to be with Daniel at the hospital in Boston, even if all she could do was sit next to him and wait. She had to be with him.

Someone must have given Daniel a ride to the ferry. After crossing Vineyard Sound, he would have taken the Peter Pan bus from Woods Hole to Boston. It was the same bus Nora took. The bus went straight to South Station, where you could get on the T, which was Boston's subway. Clem had never been to Massachusetts General Hospital, but she had ridden the subway many times. She knew there was a stop on the red line with that name.

She could find it.

In the parking lot, Clem looked at Mr. Willard's rusty old car. If she had the key, Clem felt sure she could drive it to the ferry. Adam had let her practice driving in empty parking lots back in Boston. But after the ferry ride, she'd have to drive the car all the way to Boston on the highway. She'd probably kill herself, and maybe someone else, too. So that wasn't a real option.

Then she thought of Nora's car. Nora parked her Dart in the same spot on a back street in Vineyard Haven when she took the ferry. It would be there now. Clem knew she kept a roll of cash in the driver-side ashtray. Just for emergencies.

It might be enough money to get Clem to the hospital in Boston. She needed a ferry ticket and a bus ticket, and some money for the subway in Boston. And whatever else came up.

She checked her watch. Five o'clock. If she hurried, she could still catch the ferry and then a bus from Woods Hole to Boston tonight.

But first she had to get to Vineyard Haven and find Nora's car. She walked out to the road and, almost right away, heard a car. Clem turned and stuck out her thumb.

Nora's car was just where it always was, unlocked as usual. Nobody locked their car on the Island.

Clem got in, opened the ashtray, and took out Nora's wad of bills. It felt like a lot of money. She unrolled it slowly and counted. There was a twenty, a ten, a five, and sixteen ones. Fifty-one dollars. She knew the ferry was $3.75 and she thought the bus was $17. The subway cost ninety cents. She didn't even need to add it all up. She had plenty.

30

Emergency

When Clem came out of the subway station in Boston, the hospital was right there. The big white building loomed in front of her, glowing in the dark like it was radiating heat. She followed the signs to the main entrance.

The inside seemed more like a hotel lobby than a hospital. Or maybe a shopping mall. There were stores and lots of cushioned seats. Signs pointed this way and that and people passed through in all directions. There were women in nurses' uniforms and men in white lab coats with name tags on their pockets. Patients walked by wearing pajamas or bathrobes. One man gripped an upright pole with a clear plastic bag hanging from it.

Clem stood in one place and turned slowly around, looking for Daniel.

She was nervous about asking for help. What if they asked

for her parents? But there was nothing else she could do. She walked up to the information desk. The receptionist had a telephone receiver pressed to her ear. She looked at Clem and held up a finger.

"One moment, please," she said into the phone, and pressed the "hold" button. She set the receiver down on the table. "Can I help you?"

"I'm looking for a patient."

"Name?"

"Bartholomew Willard."

The woman typed on a computer keyboard and peered at a small screen. "Can you spell that, please?"

"W–I–L–L–A–R–D."

"I don't see anybody by that name."

"They flew him in from Martha's Vineyard last night."

"Oh." Her eyes crinkled sympathetically. "You'd better try Emergency." She pointed to a hallway on her right.

"Thanks." Clem hurried down the hall, then down three more, following the sign for "Emergency" at each intersection. It was like a maze. She arrived at the ER breathless and hurried over to the receptionist's desk.

"Willard," she said. "W–I–L–L–A–R–D. He came in last night or this morning on the helicopter."

"Let's take a look." The woman looked at a clipboard in

front of her. "He's not in the ER right now. Let me check the register from the morning shift."

She opened a notebook, ran her finger down a page.

"I don't see . . . oh, wait. I—oh."

The woman looked up at Clem sadly.

"Bartholomew Willard? Transferred from Martha's Vineyard Hospital?"

Clem nodded.

"I'm so sorry, hon. It says here that he . . . well, he passed. He came in at 3:40 a.m. DOA—dead on arrival."

31

Nobody Knew

No.

That was all she could think. No. Clem backed away from the desk.

The receptionist looked at her with a worried expression. "Are you okay, dear?"

Clem shook her head. Mr. Willard had been there, every afternoon, while she and Daniel did homework at the big table. Sitting in his reading chair by the stove. Smoking his pipe. Telling them about cranberries and beetlebung trees and Rachel Carson.

He couldn't be dead.

"Honey, do you want me to call someone?" The receptionist picked up the receiver, her hand poised to dial.

Mr. Willard was Daniel's only family. Now he didn't have anybody. Except her.

Clem took a step back towards the desk. "Was there a boy here? Asking for Mr. Willard? Tall, with blond hair?"

The receptionist shook her head. Her hoop earrings swayed and banged against her neck. "Not while I've been here. I came on at three o'clock. If he came earlier, I wouldn't know. Do you want me to page him?"

"Yes, please. His name is Daniel Willard."

The woman pressed a button and spoke into the phone, and Clem heard her voice boom through the lobby. "Would Daniel Willard please report to reception? Daniel Willard."

"You can wait over there." The woman pointed to a row of upholstered seats.

Clem sat. She didn't know what she was going to say to Daniel. She glanced around the room nervously.

But as the minutes ticked by, she began to think maybe he wasn't here at all. He must have found out about his grandfather hours ago. She didn't think he knew anyone in Boston, so he would have been alone. What would he have done?

She tried to do the math in her head. There were only four ferries a day. Daniel could have come over on the first boat, and taken the bus to the hospital like she did, then found out about his grandfather. After that, he might still have been able to get a ferry back to the Island.

Maybe. She hated thinking of Daniel going home to that empty house. If he tried to call her, no one would answer. It made her even sadder to think he might not call. She'd been so mean and angry the last time they saw each other.

"He hasn't responded." The receptionist waved Clem back towards the desk. "Let me call someone for you, honey. Your parents?"

Clem stood up. "No, it's okay."

Daniel would have been upset, and confused. Maybe he didn't go home. If he wasn't in the hospital, he would have gone out and started to walk. That's what Daniel did. He liked to move.

She would look for him.

"Miss!" The receptionist stared at her. She still had the phone in her hand.

Clem turned and began to walk away. It was almost ten o'clock. Too late to catch a ferry back to the Island. She was stranded in Boston until tomorrow morning. If she had to stay, she was going to look for Daniel.

She looked back and saw the receptionist still watching her, with the phone pressed to her ear. She might be calling hospital security. Or the police. Clem forced a smile, then lifted her backpack to her shoulder and walked quickly toward the emergency room doors.

Don't run, she told herself. Don't attract attention.

Outside the hospital, a cold drizzle was falling. The rain made fuzzy halos around the white lights in the parking lot.

She shivered and buttoned her coat. She didn't have a hat.

Maybe, if she could do the same things Daniel might have done, she would find him.

Clem started across the parking lot. She didn't know where she was headed, but she was leaving the hospital. Daniel would definitely not want to stay there. Not with his grandfather dead and all the bright lights and people bustling around. He would leave.

An ambulance screamed into the parking lot, lights flashing. It honked as Clem almost stepped right in front of it. She jumped back with a gasp. "Pay attention!" she told herself. She needed to think like a city girl now. She took some deep breaths and continued on.

When she reached Charles Street, she stopped and waited for a break in the stream of cars. Then she raced across, barely making it before a tractor-trailer whizzed by. Clem started walking again, away from the traffic.

A block away, the streets narrowed and the traffic disappeared. Old brick houses were packed tightly together. This was Beacon Hill, one of the oldest parts of Boston. She had been here with her fifth-grade class to visit the State House and walk the Freedom Trail. It was pretty, she remembered.

But not at night.

At night, it was dark and shadowy. When she got a block away from Cambridge Street, the noise of the cars died away and her footsteps echoed in the deserted streets. Old gas street lamps cast dim circles of yellow light. Brick houses and apartment buildings pushed up against the sidewalk. Each doorway was a black, shadowy hole. She walked faster when she passed them.

Clem felt confused. Daniel could be anywhere. It was crazy to think she could find him.

She wondered if anyone would be looking for her yet. Tonight it was Adam's turn to call and check in. He would have telephoned the cottage at 8:30 p.m.—over an hour and a half ago—but when Clem didn't pick up, he probably just figured she was asleep or outside. He wouldn't worry.

Nora would have no idea Clem had even left the house— much less left the Island.

So nobody knew she was gone.

Her fingers felt stiff and cold. She saw crackly ice forming on puddles. The drizzle had stopped, but her hair and coat were damp. She felt shivery and her stomach growled. She hadn't eaten anything since lunch.

She arrived at a little park with a bench under a maple tree. Grateful for a chance to rest, she sat and looked up at the spreading branches. The maple probably gave wonderful shade in summer. Right now, the bare branches were tipped with tiny buds. Clem found the buds comforting.

She had been stupid to take off without a plan. Clem had

no idea where she was going to sleep. Maybe she could sit on the bench all night or walk around the streets.

That didn't seem safe.

If she went back to the bus station, she could catch a bus back to Woods Hole in the morning. Bus stations stayed open all night, and it would be warm. Maybe the Burger King would still be open. The first bus to Woods Hole was probably really early. If she got home before Nora got back, her mother might never even know she'd been away.

But the Greyhound Station was next to a seedy neighborhood called the Combat Zone. Everybody knew you were supposed to stay away from there. There were muggers and prostitutes and bars with names like "The Teddy Bare Lounge" and "The Naked Eye." If Beacon Hill was scary at night, the bus station would be ten times worse.

As if to underline her thoughts, a police siren wailed in the distance. She listened as the sound grew louder and then faded away.

She could call Nora.

Nora wasn't far away at all. The friend she stayed with on Tuesdays lived in the Back Bay, which was right next to Beacon Hill. Clem had the number. It was written on an index card that she kept in the pocket of her backpack. She'd been carrying it all year, although she'd never needed to use it. She just needed to find a pay phone.

But then she'd have to tell Nora everything. Clem didn't want to have to explain how she'd taken Nora's money and hitchhiked and traveled to Boston and ended up alone in the city at night.

A sudden rustling sound behind her startled Clem. She leapt to her feet and she walked away, fast. Her heart was pounding so loudly she could hardly think. She rounded a corner and saw a bus shelter. Someone lurked in the shadowy corner of the shelter.

Clem veered across the street, walking even faster.

She rounded another corner and forced herself to slow down. Running would make her look scared and vulnerable. A man in an overcoat came toward her on the sidewalk. It was too late to cross the street, so she ducked her head. She didn't want him to see how frightened she was.

He continued past her.

She lifted her head and saw a police car idling at a stop sign just ahead. Clem paused, then turned away. Teenagers weren't supposed to be out this late. Boston had a curfew.

Half a block later, Clem looked back over her shoulder to see if the police car had moved. That's when she slipped on the ice and fell.

She landed on her hand first. It skittered across the icy patch before scraping on pavement. Then her butt hit the ground, then her head.

Clem lay still for a moment before slowly lifting her head. Her mouth filled with the coppery taste of blood. Her hand felt numb. She sat up and felt dizzy.

In the dim gaslight, she saw bloody scrapes covering her palm. She looked around. The street was empty. No one to help her, but no one to run from either. Clem slumped over, cradling her arm.

She would never find Daniel.

She had nowhere to go.

She felt broken, inside and out. But there was no one to help her.

Clem scrambled stiffly to her feet. She stretched her arms and rolled her head and shoulders. Everything seemed to work. Her hip was bruised but she could walk, limping just a little. Her hand stung and ached. She found an old napkin in her backpack and pressed down on her palm, trying to stop the bleeding.

She went three blocks before she found a telephone booth. Clem fished out the index card with Nora's contact information. Under the telephone number and address for her office at the university, Nora had written "*MIRANDA,*" then an address on Bay State Road and a telephone number.

She stepped into the phone booth, pushed the folding door shut with her foot and dropped her backpack on the floor. She picked up the heavy black receiver and held it to her ear. It smelled of cigarette smoke. She slipped a dime into the coin slot and dialed.

The phone rang. And rang. Clem waited for ten rings and hung up.

She leaned her head against the glass wall of the phone booth and closed her eyes, for just a moment. Then she picked up the receiver again and dialed another number. Adam could help. He would find a way to get in touch with Nora. Then her mother would come get her.

"Ninety cents, please," sang the operator.

Clem dug into her pocket and stuffed more change into the slot. On the other end, the phone began to ring. Seven rings. Eight. Nine. She was about to hang up when Adam answered.

"Clem?" his voice was furry with sleep. "I tried to call you but you didn't pick up. Were you out?"

"Yes."

"I'm glad you called. I wasn't able to reach Nora either, and I was worried."

"I'm okay," she said, realizing that Adam thought she was calling from home. She needed to explain that she was stranded in Boston. But suddenly there was something else Clem wanted to ask him even more. "Adam?"

"Clem. What's going on?"

Just tell him, she thought. Tell him the whole story. Maybe Adam could make it all better.

She took a deep breath. "You know my friend, Daniel?"

"The one with the birds?"

"His grandfather died and I'm afraid they're going to take him away and he has to stay on the Island. He's trying to save the ospreys, and he can't live anywhere else. He needs help. He needs us! We can help him. He's great, you'd really like him . . ."

"Clementine! Slow down!"

"But we have to help him. Daniel doesn't have anywhere to go!"

Adam didn't say anything.

"Adam?"

"Sunshine, the thing is . . . the thing is . . . I'm not coming back to Boston. They offered me a position here at Ohio State, Clem, and I'm going to accept it. I was going to tell you in a couple of weeks, when I came to visit."

"So we're moving to Ohio?"

"I don't know."

Clem's throat tightened. "Don't you want us to come live with you?"

"Well." Adam hesitated. "That's up to your mother."

"What do you mean?" she whispered. "Are you . . . splitting up?"

"I think so, sweetie." Adam was whispering, too.

For a long minute, neither of them said anything. Then the recorded voice of the operator broke in.

"Please deposit seventy cents for the next three minutes. Please deposit seventy cents."

"Clementine? CLEM? Are you calling from a pay phone? Where are you? CLEM!"

Clem didn't have seventy cents. And she didn't have anything else to say to Adam. She hung up the phone.

She reached into her pocket and pulled out the remaining change. A couple of nickels, a penny, and a subway token. Thank God. There was just one place it could take her, and she knew the way.

32

Like You Could Walk on Water

The door opened to the apartment opened. Coco's mother stood there in a silky white robe.

"*Clementina?*" She looked shocked. "What are you doing here?"

Clem shook her head. She was wet and chilled through and she didn't know what to say.

"Mom? What's all the noise?" Coco, in bare legs and a baggy T-shirt, appeared behind her mother. "Clem?"

She grabbed Clem's arm and pulled her into the apartment. "You're freezing! What happened? Are you okay?"

Clem nodded and let her backpack fall to the floor of the living room. "I'm sorry. I'm really sorry. I didn't know where else to go."

"Sit down, *pobrecita*," said Mrs. Braverman. "Let me have a look at that hand. What did you do? Where's Nora?"

"I don't know." Clem winced as Coco's mom peeled away the bloody napkin and examined Clem's hand. "I tried to call her. She doesn't know I'm in Boston."

"How did you get here?" Coco's mother asked.

The story seemed too big for Clem to explain. "I came by myself. I was trying to find somebody." She looked at Coco, whose eyes were wide. "I couldn't find him. I don't know where he is." She started to cry. "And Nora and Adam are . . ."

Mrs. Braverman put an arm around Clem's shoulders. "Don't worry, dear. It will be fine."

"But it won't!" Clem shook her head fiercely. "It won't be!" She saw Coco and her mother exchange a worried glance.

"Come into the kitchen, where the phone is," said Mrs. Braverman. "You should try to call Nora again. I'm sure your mother can help."

Clem shook her head. She did not want to talk to her mother right now.

"I am glad you came here," Mrs. Braverman said. "Coco is too, right?" She looked at Coco. "We've missed you around here all year. But what you need right now is to rest. Why don't you give me Nora's number? I will try to call. You two girls should go right to bed."

Clem pulled the index card out of her backpack.

Mrs. Braverman took the card and looked at it. "Go wash that hand. Pour some hydrogen peroxide on it. Coco knows where everything is."

"C'mon, Clem." Coco grabbed her backpack. "I'll find you a toothbrush."

Fifteen minutes later, Clem was nestled in the familiar cocoon of Coco's room, lying on her futon, covered by a pile of quilts. The last thing she remembered was Coco bustling around. She dropped off to sleep.

"Wake up, Island Girl."

Clem opened her eyes.

Coco crouched next to her. "I get to play hooky today so we can take you to the bus station later."

Clem closed her eyes again for a second, then struggled to a sitting position. Coco plunked down cross-legged beside her on the futon.

"Clem. What's going on?"

"It's Daniel. His grandfather died. I don't know where he went."

"What is it with that boy?"

"Don't be like that. You're my friend."

"I used to think so."

Clem studied Coco's face and was surprised to see that her expression was not mean, or even angry. Coco looked hurt. Clem had hurt her.

"I'm sorry," she said. "I'm sorry I embarrassed you at that party."

Coco looked away. "Like I cared. That guy was a terrible kisser. But the way you looked at me after, in the car? It made me feel like . . . like dirt."

"I didn't mean to make you feel bad. I was just surprised, you know? I never saw you drink before, and when you went off with that guy, I—"

"Oh my God, that beer was gross!" Coco shook her head, then leaned back against the wall with a thunk. "I'm such a show-off. To be honest, I'm glad you dragged me out of there. I don't even know what I was doing with that guy. I think I was just bummed out about Ricky."

She peeked over at Clem. "I might have been bumming about you and Daniel, too."

Clem stared at Coco. "Really?"

"Clem, the way he looked at you, like you could walk on water or something . . ."

Clem felt the blood rush to her face. "Wait. You? You were jealous?"

"Well, maybe just a little." Coco sighed. "I wasn't even that excited about the party. I just wanted to get you away from Daniel."

"Well, you don't have to worry about that now."

"What are you talking about?"

Clem shook her head.

"Clem. What is going on? You wouldn't say anything last night. Now you have to tell me what happened." Coco pounded a pillow to puff it up, tossed it on the futon and lay down.

Clem did the same. They lay shoulder to shoulder, staring up at the Donna Summer poster tacked to Coco's ceiling. The singer's long, wild curls looked like Coco's hair.

The poster was new, but it felt a little like old times.

She told Coco everything then, starting with the moment she saw the osprey. Only a day had passed, but it seemed like it had happened days ago. Weeks, maybe. Coco listened without interrupting until Clem finished the story.

"So that's how you found out about your parents? Adam just spilled his guts?" Coco asked.

"Pretty much," said Clem. "He didn't know I was in Boston. He didn't mean to do it that way."

"And what happens now?"

"Adam wants to stay in Ohio. I don't know what we'll do. They haven't told me anything." Clem felt her anger returning. "Nothing."

"I know a kid who spends one week with his mom and one week with his dad. They all live in Cambridge. But maybe you could do something like that."

"Back and forth. Like the ospreys." Clem shook her head. "That would be crazy."

They were quiet for a minute.

"So, last night, when you didn't know where to go," said Coco. "Why didn't you come straight here?"

"I thought you hated me," said Clem.

Coco rolled over to face her and propped herself up on one elbow. "I was mad, I'll give you that," she said. "But I could never hate you. Never."

Clem turned her head then to meet Coco's eyes, and saw she was telling the truth. "Me neither," she said.

Coco lay back on the bed. "Nora was really upset when Mom finally got ahold of her. She already knew you were missing because Adam called her. We're going to meet her at the bus station at ten thirty so you guys can go back to the Vineyard together."

Clem looked over at Coco's bedside clock. It was 9:05 a.m. "I don't know if I want to see Nora."

"You kind of have to."

"But I never found Daniel. I still don't know where he is."

"I have a feeling Daniel's pretty good at looking out for himself. I bet he's okay."

When they got to the bus station, Nora was waiting near the ticket counter. She looked pale.

"Oh, sweetie, I'm so glad you're all right!" She took Clem's face in her hands. "You are all right, aren't you?"

Clem nodded.

"I feel terrible that you couldn't reach me. Miranda unplugged the phone when she took a nap yesterday and forgot to plug it back in. I had no idea you were calling!"

Clem didn't say anything.

"I think she's exhausted," Mrs. Braverman said to Nora. "Let's go find your gate and make sure you two don't miss your bus."

"I got our tickets already," said Nora. "Gate 23."

They made their way to the gate, where the bus was waiting, its engine idling.

"Thank you so much, Lorena," said Nora. "I feel very, very lucky that you and Coco were there for Clem last night."

"It is my pleasure," said Coco's mom. She smiled warmly at Clem.

Clem went to give Coco a hug and saw that she was crying. Her strong, cool friend.

"Don't do that, you," she whispered, and closed her eyes while Coco enveloped her in a warm, sweet-smelling embrace. "I'll see you soon."

"You better," Coco answered.

33

We Need to Talk

Clem pressed her hand against the window as the bus backed out of its slot. Coco waved at her. Even after the bus had pulled away from the station, Clem kept her face turned toward the window.

Nora put a hand on her knee. "We need to talk."

"I know," said Clem. "I just . . . can we talk when we get home? I feel so tired."

"All right." Nora removed her hand. "When you're ready." She pulled a thick book out of the bag between her feet and paged through it, looking for her place.

For the next hour, Clem sat with her cheek pressed against the cold glass of the window while her neck and shoulder grew numb. Boston slipped away, and Dorchester, and the warehouses and motels at the city's edge. It was all familiar. The three of them had traveled this road together so many times on the way to the Vineyard. Now it was just her and Nora.

In her secret heart of hearts, Clem had always thought that maybe she loved Adam a little bit more than she loved Nora. He was so much fun while Nora was serious. But right now, Nora was here and Adam wasn't.

As the bus crossed the Bourne Bridge over the Cape Cod Canal, Clem reached into her backpack and pulled out *Silent Spring*. She opened to the first chapter, "A Fable for Tomorrow." It told the story of a little town where poisonous chemicals had gotten into the environment.

First, the chickens and farm animals perished. Plants and trees wasted away. People began reporting strange illnesses. Some children died.

And then, all the birds disappeared. And so did their songs. Their chattering, their chirping, their calling in the early morning and high overhead at the water's edge. All silenced. This was the "Silent Spring" of the book's title.

Clem shivered. The first time she read the chapter, back in November, she could hardly imagine it.

Yet, sitting here now, unable to talk to Nora, with Adam disappearing in the distance and Mr. Willard gone and Daniel somewhere out of reach, she found she *could* imagine it. This was how Clem's life felt right now. A silent, disturbing place.

She thought about the family camping trips, summers on the Vineyard, potluck suppers at their Cambridge apartment.

Sitting at the kitchen table with Nora's or Adam's students and listening to them talk about politics, music, and the war in Vietnam. She thought about Mr. Willard leaning back in his chair to begin another story, and Daniel catching her eye across the battered table as they both prepared to listen.

Nothing would bring those days back. Nothing. They were gone forever.

At Woods Hole, Clem got off the bus and went to the bathroom while Nora bought the ferry tickets. Then they boarded the ferry. Clem usually loved the crossing, but today was different. The brisk ocean air felt cold and damp. She choked on the tarry diesel exhaust as she climbed the steel staircase to the upper deck. Then Clem stood at the railing and watched as the harbor slipped by and the houses along the shore got smaller and smaller.

The choppy sea looked gray and oily. The wind whipped her hair into tangled strings that cut across her face. Gulls swooped behind the boat and called out to her, hoping she would toss them a chip or some bread as so many passengers often did. The birds made her think of Daniel. Was he at his house now, all alone, wondering what came next?

"Hi." Nora joined her at the railing. Her face looked sad.

"Hey," said Clem.

Nora put her arm around Clem's shoulder. Clem wanted to relax against her, but she couldn't. She felt stiff.

"I talked to Adam. He told me about your phone call. That's not the way I wanted you to find out."

Clem looked down at the chipped paint of the boat railing.

"I am so sorry. Adam and I have tried. We really have. But we've each become very different people than we were when we married. And we just don't belong together anymore."

At that moment, Clem realized that she had known this for a long time. Maybe even since Christmas. Or Thanksgiving. A part of her had hoped that something would happen to keep her family together. That Nora would decide to move there, too, or that Adam would change his mind and come home.

Clem felt cold. Not even angry anymore. Just cold.

"What about me?" she asked.

Nora stroked her hair. For one long minute, Clem pretended she was still small and her powerful, comforting mother could make everything better.

"We'll stay in Cambridge. Or on the Island. You can visit Adam as often as we can make it work. We'll both still be with you. We just won't all be in the same place."

34

Right Here

Clem found Daniel waiting at the cottage.

He sat at the kitchen table with *Birds of North America* lying open in front of him. He looked up at her, his blue eyes rimmed in red, then stood. Clem walked straight to him and put her arms around him. At first he seemed embarrassed and stiff, his arms hanging helplessly at his sides.

Then, slowly, he wrapped his arms around her and held on tight.

"Where did you go?" he whispered. "I've been waiting and waiting."

"I went to the hospital in Boston," said Clem. "To find you."

"Oh, Clem," he said, "I've been here the whole time."

"Right here?" Clem stepped back and looked up at him.

"I stayed last night at Bo's. But I've been calling. Bo

brought me over this morning to wait for you when he heard you were coming home."

"So you never left the Island?"

"They wouldn't let me go to Boston with Grandfather," he said. "One of the doctors at the hospital told me he would drive me there at the end of his shift. So I waited for him in town. But before his shift ended, he got word from Boston that Grandfather was—well—I suppose you know."

"I'm so sorry." Clem pulled him into a hug again. "I'm sorry I wasn't there."

He rested his cheek against her hair. His shoulders shook a little. She caught a faint scent of pipe tobacco on his clothes. Clem held him tighter.

"They're going to bring Grandfather back here to be buried on the Vineyard," Daniel said.

"That's good," Clem whispered into the collar of his jacket.

They sat across from each other at the table and Nora brought them bowls of soup. Daniel had purple-blue shadows beneath his eyes. Clem wondered if he had slept at all. They ate in silence, then brought their empty bowls to Nora at the sink.

"Let's go outside," said Clem.

Daniel followed her onto the porch. They sat side by side on the steps.

"Tell me everything," said Clem.

Daniel told her that he had awakened in the night to find his grandfather moaning in pain. How he thought of calling 911 but there didn't seem enough time for an ambulance to find its way to where they were and then all the way down-island to the hospital. So he'd bundled his grandfather into the car and taken him there himself.

"Do you know how to drive?"

Daniel smiled at that, although it was a sad smile. "It's funny what you find out you can do when you need to," he said.

Once he got to the hospital, the orderlies took his grandfather away and Daniel was left waiting. Then they told him Mr. Willard was going to be flown to Boston.

"Clem, I didn't even get to say goodbye." Daniel's chin quivered and his eyes filled. Then he collected himself and went on.

After he got the news about his grandfather, Daniel called Bo. "He took me to his house. After three thirty, when I thought you would get home from school, I started calling, but you didn't answer."

"I was on my way to Boston then!"

"I was so worried about you, Clem—I had no idea what could have happened. Then this morning, Jill called Bo and told him you were coming home."

"Jill?"

"She got a call from Mrs. Braverman. I think she said she found Jill's number in your backpack."

She remembered the slip of paper Jill had given her at school. Coco's mother must have looked in her bag when she was sleeping, probably because she couldn't reach Nora. So many people had been worried about her—Nora, Adam, Daniel, Bo, Jill, Coco's mom. She felt a little ashamed. At the same time, she was grateful.

"When I knew you were coming home, I asked Bo to bring me back here. I've been waiting here ever since," said Daniel. "Did you really go to Boston looking for me?"

"Yes." Now it was Clem's turn to tell her story, about taking the boat and the bus and going to the hospital and walking the city streets at night and slipping on the ice.

And also about her phone call to Adam.

"It feels so weird," she said. "We were always a family. Now I don't know what we are."

Then she stopped, afraid of how her words might be affecting Daniel. He'd never had that kind of family at all—not in memory, anyway. But he put his arm around her and leaned in.

"You're still a family," he said. "They still love you."

"I wish they loved each other."

Daniel nodded and looked up at the darkening sky.

Clem looked up, too. A crow passed overhead, cawing loudly. It landed on a branch of the big tree.

"I saw an osprey," she blurted out. "At Menemsha."

"You did?" Daniel straightened. "Bo told me a few people had called him to report sightings."

"I thought it might be Noepe."

"It might be," he said.

As they sat watching the crow, Bo rattled up the driveway in his truck.

Nora stepped out onto the porch.

"Evening, Mrs. Harper," said Bo, getting out of the truck.

"Bo, you know you can call me Nora. I hear you looked after Daniel last night."

"Yep, and I'm getting ready to take him back there now, if he's ready. I'll bring him back to you tomorrow, Miss Clem, so you can catch up. But right now I think this boy should get some sleep."

"I agree," said Nora.

"I am tired," said Daniel, looking at Clem. "But I'll be back."

35

How Mother Nature Made Us

Clem slept late the next day, even though it was a Thursday.

"Maybe you should take Friday off, too," said Nora. "Start fresh next week."

She was sitting on the steps when Bo dropped Daniel off around eleven o'clock. Bo waved at Clem and backed away down the drive. She studied Daniel's face as he loped toward her. He still looked tired, but his face was lighter. Less worried.

"What did you guys do?" she asked.

"We went back to his house and fed the birds. Ate some dinner with Jill. Then we talked. Bo had a lot of stuff to tell me. Or, rather, to ask me."

"Like what?"

"Bo wants to adopt me, Clem. Or maybe become my foster father. Whatever the court says he can do. He wants me to come live with him."

Clem stared. "Really? Do you want to do that?"

"Yes," said Daniel. "I think I do. Bo said it's not for sure, since it all has to be approved. But he seemed hopeful."

"What about Jill?" Clem asked.

Daniel smiled a little. "That's kind of a secret, but I can tell you. They're going to get married."

Clem's mouth dropped open. "So Jill would be like your mom?"

Daniel shrugged, but didn't stop smiling.

"That's so great," she said, giving him an awkward little hug. She hoped he couldn't see the confusion she felt. Even though she was happy for him, she was also a little jealous. Daniel would end up with a happy family . . . while hers was falling apart.

When she stepped back, Daniel looked at her seriously.

"We talked about Quitsa and Noepe's nest, too," he said. "Bo hasn't been able to find another good location nearby. He's taking down the nesting platform so Noepe will look somewhere else."

"But she might go far away," said Clem. "Maybe even off the Island!"

"I know." Daniel kicked a little stone away from the steps. "She'll find a good place, though. I know she will."

Clem still wanted Noepe to raise a family here. On Martha's

Vineyard. On Cobb's Lane, if possible. She wanted to be there when it happened.

"Don't you think we could still stop Mrs. Brewster? We could . . . I don't know . . . lie down in front of the bulldozers!"

"Clementine." Daniel gave her a long look.

"I know, I know. That would be kind of crazy. But we can't do nothing!"

"We're out of time. And we've done everything we can think of."

"We could have protested. Why didn't you stick up for me that day? When I was handing out the fliers? And Beth turned everyone against me?"

"Clem, I'm sorry about that," he said. "I don't think I could have changed their minds, but I should have stood by you."

"That would have helped."

Daniel shook his head. "It wasn't about who's lived on the Island longer, or who's allowed to have an opinion. They were wrong.

"But Clem, Mrs. Brewster is going to build that house. It's her land. The birds have to find another home, whether it's this year or next year." Daniel looked down at the ground. "We need to knock this home down so the birds will go find a better one."

"Bo can cut it down if he wants," she said. "I'll stay home."

"You can do that, if it's what you want to do," he said. "But I helped put that platform up. I'm going to help take it down."

Bo returned with Jill in his truck later that afternoon. Clem stood in the yard and watched as Daniel climbed in back.

"C'mon, Clem," Bo yelled from the cab.

She shook her head.

Bo said something to Jill, then jumped down from the driver's seat. He walked over across the yard to stand next to Clem. "First of all, I want to thank you."

"Thank me? For what?"

"I want to thank you for goin' to look for Daniel. He doesn't have too many folks who would just pick up and run off like that to help him out."

"I—I was just worried about him."

"I know! He needs people to worry about him."

Clem shook her head. "Well, it was a total mistake. He wasn't even there."

"That's not the point. You did what you thought was needed to help him and I thank you for it."

Clem nodded. Bo's words made her feel a little better about her trip to Boston. Like she had done one thing right.

"I'm thinking you don't want to come help take down Quitsa and Noepe's nesting pole. That right?"

She nodded. "I don't even want to watch."

"I know you wanted to save the birds' home. Because you care about them. To be honest, it's a big disappointment for me, takin' down that pole. I put it up."

Clem studied Bo's weathered face. His kind eyes were steady and she felt like he could see her thoughts.

"But trying to keep a nest that's no good for the birds won't help 'em, Clem. In fact, it'll hurt. What Noepe needs right now is for us to stop helping. We gotta trust that she'll know what to do."

"But what if she doesn't know?"

"We're all survivors, Clem. Mother Nature made us that way. Look at Quinn—he lost his daddy and his mom abandoned him. But he survived. And you know what? Noepe will, too."

Clem thought about Quinn. After his family fell apart, Quinn had found a place to live and grow up. He might even have a mate by now.

"Know what I'm saying, Clem?"

She nodded. People and birds were alike. Things happened that hurt them or made their lives harder. All the time. But losing someone or something important didn't mean the end of everything. It meant you had to find a new way to do things.

Bo turned and walked toward the pickup. "Come on then. This is gonna be tough for all of us. We can use your help."

When they reached the nesting pole, an osprey was already perched on the edge of the nest. Daniel and Clem jumped down from the truck and walked over, staring up at the huge bird. The osprey looked right back at them, turning its head this way and that.

"Kew-kew-kew-kew-kew!"

"Is it Noepe?" she asked.

"I don't know—I can't see its legs," Daniel answered. "What do you think, Bo?"

In one hand, Bo carried a bright orange chainsaw. He squinted up at the bird. "She's got the size, and she looks a little dark, the way the females do. She's a beauty. Whether it's Noepe, though, I'd have to see the bands to know."

"What if she already has eggs?" Clem asked.

"Don't worry about that," said Bo. "She just got here. She won't be ready to lay for a while. So we've gotta get her out of here. We're gonna have to make a disturbance."

"Kew-kew-kew-kew-kew!" the osprey scolded them, like she knew they were here to make trouble.

Daniel stepped forward and started waving his arms. "Get out!" he yelled. "Go!"

Clem lifted up her arms. "Go on! Out of here!" Her voice came out small and squeaky. She took a deep breath. "Go!"

The bird raised herself up at the edge of the nest. She spread her wings, almost like she was waving back at them. "*Kew-kew-kew-kew-kew!*"

"Come on," muttered Daniel. "Why won't she go?"

Bo placed his chainsaw on the ground. He put on a pair of safety goggles, then crouched over the chainsaw for a moment, manipulating the switch. "Daniel, Jill, Clem—stand back a bit."

He bent over and put one foot on the chainsaw. Reaching down, Bo grabbed a handle and pulled out the starter rope. The chainsaw rattled and then stopped. He did it again. The engine revved and died. Three more pulls, and the chainsaw roared to life. Bo lifted it up and gunned the engine. *Vroom—vroom—VROOM!*

"*Kew-kew-kew-kew-kew!*" the osprey protested. She spread and folded her wings in a jerky, agitated way. "*Kew-kew-kew!*"

"I hate to do this to you, little missy," said Bo. "But it's for your own good." He gunned the engine again and took a few steps toward the pole.

The osprey leaped from the nest, swooping down and then up into the sky. One, two, three circles overhead. Clem caught a glimpse of something on her right leg. Was it a colored band? She wasn't sure.

"Is it her, Daniel? Is it Noepe?" she hollered over the sound of the saw.

"Still can't tell," he yelled. "I wish I had my binoculars."

Then the osprey headed out toward the water, flying away from them. The bird rose higher and higher. Jill raised her arm and waved, as if the osprey could see her waving goodbye.

Bo stopped revving the saw. "That's good. She's gone off to look for another spot. Now, you three look sharp while I'm cutting. You can never be sure which way a tree will fall, and nesting poles are probably about the same."

Jill, Daniel, and Clem moved away from the pole, toward the trees. From about thirty feet away, Clem watched as Bo made a cut in the far side of the pole, then came around and sawed deep into the pole from their side. The pole vibrated. Twigs fell off the nesting platform and two small birds flew out of the lower portion of the nest.

Then the pole and platform began to sway. The nest slid this way and that. Bo cut the engine, placed one hand against the pole and pushed. Then he stepped back, carrying the saw.

"Timber," he said softly.

There was an enormous cracking noise.

As they watched together, the pole swayed one last time, then tipped. The platform and giant nest came crashing down.

36

Song of Spring

On Saturday, Clem went to the funeral for Mr. Willard at the church in Chilmark. She sat in the front pew with Daniel, Bo, Jill, and Nora. Jill brought a spray of snowdrops from her garden—the first flowers of spring. She carefully pinned them to Daniel's sweater.

To Clem's surprise, a lot of kids from school showed up—Sandy, Joe, Daisy, even Beth. They'd dressed up for the service, and their faces were serious. Many other people filled the pews. Clem even spotted Mrs. Brewster.

She reminded herself that Mr. Willard had lived his entire life on Martha's Vineyard. He wasn't a washashore. People on the Island had known him for years and years.

Clem sat next to Daniel, close enough for their arms to touch. He hardly moved and didn't look at anyone. He stared down at his shoes or up at the stained glass window in the front of the church. During the minister's eulogy for Mr. Willard, Clem reached over and grabbed his hand. He squeezed and didn't let go.

Afterward, there was a reception in the church social hall with lemonade and cookies. Everybody stood around talking in quiet voices. Clem noticed that Bo had taken up a watchful position near Daniel—like they were on the same football team and he was ready to block for him or run interference.

Sandy walked over and handed Clem a plate with two sugar cookies on it. "I know you spent a lot of time with Daniel's grandfather," she said. "I'm sorry."

"Thanks."

"And Clem? About my grandma . . ."

Clem cut her off. "I'm sorry if I made you mad about the protest. I didn't know—"

"No! It's okay." Sandy looked around, then lowered her voice. "I wanted to help but I couldn't."

"Really?"

"I tried to get her to change her mind. But it was useless. My grandma is a really determined kind of person. That's how come she's so successful. But you can't tell her anything." Sandy rolled her eyes.

Clem felt surprised and glad to hear that Sandy had taken her side against Mrs. Brewster.

Sandy nudged her. "Look over there."

Beth was walking toward Daniel. Clem's first thought was to run over and stop her before she could say something mean to him. But then Beth reached out and put her arms around Daniel. And as she did, Clem glimpsed her face.

Beth's eyes were swollen and her nose was red and shiny. She'd been crying.

"Wow," said Sandy. "She's human after all."

The next morning, Clem woke up early. Daniel had come for dinner after the funeral and ended up sleeping on their couch. She opened her bedroom door and peeked into the living room. Daniel slept on his side under a blue quilt, his face half-crushed against his outstretched arm. His hair stuck out in all directions and one long leg, still in jeans, hung over the side of the couch.

She tiptoed in and sat down in the old armchair opposite him. His chest rose and fell gently. The pink color had come back into his cheeks. Clem felt like she could watch him sleep for a very long time.

His eyes fluttered open. "Is it morning?"

"Yes." Clem looked out the window at the pinkening sky. "Almost morning, anyway."

Daniel sat up. He ran a hand through his tousled hair. As he looked around the cottage, Clem saw his expression change from confusion to dejection. His eyes, so bright at first seeing her when they opened, clouded over. His face seemed to sag.

He was remembering.

"Want to go for a walk?" she said. "It's the most beautiful time of the day."

Daniel hesitated, and she saw his face change again. He was pulling himself together.

"You're right, it is," he said. "Also the best time to see birds."

"I'll be right back." Clem went back to her bedroom. She put on jeans and hiking shoes and brushed her teeth. When she stepped back into the living room, Daniel was lacing up his boots. He picked up her binoculars and slung them around his neck.

As they stepped outside the cottage, Clem felt like something had changed. The air was still cold, but the damp woods no longer seemed dreary and dead. A few of the trees—just a few—had sprouted tiny green leaves. Tattered dead leaves still covered the ground, but the tips of little green shoots peeked out of the soil. It wasn't spring yet, but winter was nearly over.

They walked quietly together along Cobb's Lane and then through the woods along Daniel's shortcut. Clem breathed deeply, tasting the fresh air. In the distance, she heard a gentle chirping noise that sounded like baby birds. But it was the middle of March.

"Can you hear those poor hatchlings? They'll freeze to death," Clem said.

Daniel stopped to listen. "That's not a bird—it's a little frog. A pinkletink."

Clem laughed. "That is a ridiculous name."

"I know," said Daniel. "Some people call them spring peepers, but Vineyarders call them pinkletinks. People get excited when they hear them because it means winter is over. Grandfather called it the song of spring."

As they stepped out of the woods, Clem saw that Daniel had led them to the place where they had cut down the nesting platform yesterday. All that remained of the pole was a neat stack of logs. If Noepe returned here now, she wouldn't see her nest—only a bare spot in a clearing.

She gazed out over the water. The ocean was gray, but the sunrise cast glints of light like confetti on its surface.

"Clem! Look!" Daniel said, pointing upward.

Shading her eyes with her hand, she scanned the sky.

High above the waves, an osprey soared in slow, easy circles, its tail fanned and its striped wings spread wide.

Daniel looked through the binoculars, then passed them to her. Clem raised the binoculars to her eyes and found the osprey. Following a flying bird was hard, but she caught a glimpse of the bird's legs. Two bands. She lowered the binoculars and looked at Daniel.

He smiled his crooked smile. "It's Noepe, Clem. She's back."

Clem took a step forward, ready to chase the bird down the beach. As she watched, the osprey halted in the air, flapping slowly to stay in place, her feet outstretched. Then she dove, plunging headfirst toward the water.

With a huge splash, she disappeared beneath the surface.

Time stood still for a moment.

Then Noepe exploded out of the water in a sparkling shower of droplets. Her wings worked mightily as she pulled herself into the air. A big shining fish wriggled in her talons.

The osprey rose into the sky, headed for home, wherever that might be.

"She's beautiful," Clem said, still looking at the sky.

Daniel stood right behind her. He put his arms around her. Clem leaned back against him. She felt light-headed and wonderful and a little strange, like her insides were melting.

They stood that way for a while.

Finally Clem turned around and faced Daniel. She had to ask him something.

"I know that Noepe's going to find a place to raise a family." She gazed up at his face. "But I wish we knew where she was going. Don't you?"

Daniel looked at her intently. Then he reached down and

carefully pushed a stray strand of hair off her face, tucking it behind her ear.

"It's okay, Clem," he said. "I think she'll be okay."

"Really?" She wanted to believe it.

He paused. "Things will be okay."

She saw in his eyes that he understood. Even after everything he'd been through, Daniel knew that Clem had lost something she loved, too. He understood.

He leaned closer to her, close enough that she could feel his warm breath on her cheek.

Clem looked up into his face and imagined kissing him.

And then she did.

A Note from the Author

Clem's story is a work of fiction. But like many fictional stories, *Washashore* is rooted in fact. Martha's Vineyard is a real place that I have loved for most of my life. I have tried to be faithful to its geography in almost every case. Most of the locations in *Washashore* are real, with the exceptions of Cobb's Lane and the little peninsula where Daniel's house sits. I have also changed a few place names and details.

The characters, however, are entirely my own creations and are not based on real people—with one exception, Bo Jameson. His personal characteristics and life story are fictional, but his efforts to help the ospreys are based on the work of Gus Ben David, a naturalist who lives on Martha's Vineyard.

In 1972, when Congress banned the use of DDT for insect control, there were only two pairs of ospreys still nesting on Martha's Vineyard. That year, Gus Ben David put up the first man-made osprey pole on the Island. He wanted to provide a safe nesting place for the birds. At that time, Gus was the director of the Felix Neck Wildlife Sanctuary.

Over the next decades, Gus put up more than one hundred nesting poles on the Island. Today, Gus has retired from the sanctuary but still watches over and protects the Vineyard osprey population, which has grown to more than sixty pairs! He now runs a museum at his Vineyard home called the World of Reptiles and Birds Park. It's a lot like Bo's Bird World (but in a different location) with the addition of snakes, turtles, and lizards. It is also open to the public.

Saving the ospreys on Martha's Vineyard involved hard work by many people. Some of them live on the Island, like Gus Ben David. Some, like Rachel Carson, told the world about the dangers of pesticides. And others, such as the citizens who sued to get DDT banned, pushed the government to make things better.

We now know much more about environmental threats than when *Silent Spring* was published in 1962.

Pollution, contamination, habitat destruction, climate change—these problems are complicated and can seem overwhelming. But there are ways that you can help.

Nobody solves big problems alone; progress starts with lots of people doing something. The first step is knowing what you want to save. Before Clem found the osprey on the beach, she never thought about birds. But once she had taken home Quitsa's bands, and learned about the ospreys and DDT, and met Bo and Daniel, her world became filled with birds. Beautiful, fascinating birds. And she wanted to do something to protect them and make them safe.

For me, I want to do something about climate change—especially after I learned that rising sea levels are changing the shores and beaches I love. The beautiful colored clay cliffs that Clem and Daniel explored in *Washashore* are much smaller today because of erosion. After Blizzard Nemo hit the Island in 2013, one of the cliffs collapsed. Erosion is natural, but man-made climate change is speeding it up—and knowing that makes me want to do something about it.

What can I do? Bike instead of drive. Unplug my chargers. Use less water. Recycle. Buy compact fluorescent bulbs and turn my lights off when I don't need them. These little things are just a start, but sometimes it's surprising how much more you want to do once you get started.

Is there something that you want to save?

Suzanne Goldsmith

More about Ospreys

All About Birds. The Cornell Lab of Ornithology runs this great website full of information about birds. You can look up ospreys in the search bar. www.allaboutbirds.org

Felix Neck Wildlife Sanctuary. The Audubon Society operates this nature preserve on Martha's Vineyard. www.massaudubon.org/Nature_Connection/Sanctuaries/Felix _Neck

Rob Bierregaard is a biologist who has studied the Martha's Vineyard ospreys for decades. He tracks their migration using radio transmitters and posts reports on the ospreys' progress on his fascinating website. www.bioweb.uncc.edu/bierregaard/ospreys.htm

Ospreycams. Many nature centers have cameras on their osprey nesting. Watch between April and August/September as the birds nest, breed, and raise their young. Type "ospreycam" into your search engine and you'll find many to choose from.

Raptor Centers. There are numerous centers around the country that rescue raptors, support them in the wild, and educate the public about these wild birds. Type in "raptor center" and the name of your state to find one near you.

More about Rachel Carson

The Life and Legacy of Rachel Carson. Biographer Linda Lear provides tons of information about Carson's life and writings on this website. Lear wrote a fine biography, *Rachel Carson: Witness for Nature*, for adult readers. www.rachelcarson.org

Rachel Carson: A Twentieth-Century Life by Ellen Levine. This good biography is written for ages eleven and up, and includes excerpts from Carson's books and letters and lots of photos. It's part of the "Up Close" biography series published by Viking.

"Rachel Carson's Legacy" is a forty-three-minute video about Carson's life, based on a one-woman play by actor Kaiulani Lee. The video also includes documentary footage. This originally aired on the PBS program *Bill Moyers Journal.* View it online at: http://video.pbs.org/video/1442629512/

The House of Life: Rachel Carson at Work by Paul Brooks This is the book that Mr. Willard reads to Clem and Daniel in Chapter 14. It contains bits of biography and excerpts from Rachel Carson's books and articles. The author was Carson's editor for many years. *The House of Life* was published in 1972 by Houghton Mifflin and reprinted by Mariner Books in 1989.

More about Conservation and the Environment

A Student's Guide to Global Climate Change. This website, run by the US Environmental Protection Agency, has lots of information about climate change and its effects, as well as things you can do to help slow the process. epa.gov/climatechange/kids/

The U.S. Fish and Wildlife Service. This site has a special map where you can click on your home state and learn more about endangered species in your own backyard. It also lists ways you can help endangered species. www.fws.gov

The Vineyard Conservation Society (which does not have anyone named Emily Brewster on its board) has been working to protect the fragile ecology of Martha's Vineyard since 1965. www.vineyardconservation.org

The Audubon Society focuses on conservation of birds and wildlife. It has 500 local chapters nationwide and many centers for learning and conservation. www.audubon.org

World of Reptiles and Birds Park is Gus Ben David's nature museum, with an aviary park and reptile exhibits. If you are on Martha's Vineyard, pay him a visit! www.reptilesandbirds.com

Flying WILD encourages students to get involved in stewardship through educational programs featuring migratory birds. www.flyingwild.org

350.org offers many ways to get involved with solving the problem of climate change. This international organization has volunteers in over 188 countries. www.350.org

ABOUT THE AUTHOR

Suzanne Goldsmith grew up in Massachusetts. During high school, she lived alone in a cottage on Martha's Vineyard for a summer while working in an art gallery. She loves the Island and spends time there every summer. Suzanne is also the author of *A City Year*, a nonfiction book about an internationally-known service program based in Boston. She lives in Ohio with her family. This is her first novel.

TENT CITY

princess

Some things you keep secret from everyone . . .

Having to move into a tent after the bank repossesses your family's house is definitely one of them.

Unfortunately, fifteen-year-old Kennedy is now faced with a choice.

The City Council might tear down the tent city where she lives.

Stepping forward to save her home could cost Kennedy her friends, her boyfriend Rico, and the Battelle Young Leaders program internship that she worked all year to attain.

Should she standup for what is right . . . even if it means standing alone?

Lucky Marble Books
An Imprint of PageSpring Publishing